"You think I don't care about people——that I don't have feelings?

"Oh, I have feelings, I assure you. I may not understand you, Darcy Evans, but I've definitely noticed you. I may not always commend you for your progress, but I've seen you excel in numerous areas and have been proud of your accomplishments. Keep in mind that I'm flesh and blood—not a 'stuffed shirt,' as you call it. Why, a few times this past week I almost kissed you—" Brent broke off, his face darkening in embarrassment. Hastily he lowered his hands to his sides. "Forgive me. That was uncalled-for."

Before he could move away, Darcy spoke. "Well, why didn't you?"

He hesitated. "Why didn't I what?"

"Kiss me."

He looked uncomfortable. "Miss Evans, I strongly recommend that we cease this conversation."

**PAMELA GRIFFIN** lives in Texas and divides her time among family, church activities, and writing. She fully gave her life to the Lord in 1988 after a rebellious young adulthood and owes the fact that she's still alive today to an all-loving and forgiving God and a mother who prayed that her wayward daughter would come "home." Pamela's main goal in writing Christian romance is to encourage others through entertaining stories that also heal the wounded spirit.

Please visit Pamela at:
http://members.cowtown.net/PamelaGriffin/

Books by Pamela Griffin

**HEARTSONG PRESENTS**
HP372—'Til We Meet Again
HP420—In the Secret Place
HP446—Angels to Watch Over Me
HP469—Beacon of Truth
HP520—The Flame Within

# Heart
# Appearances

*Pamela Griffin*

*Heartsong Presents*

As always I dedicate this book to my Lord Jesus, who looks beyond my imperfect outer shell to the loving heart that seeks only to serve Him. Also, thanks to my critique partners, who are always so willing to lend a hand. You girls are truly the best, and I never could have done it without you.

**A note from the Author:**
I love to hear from my readers! You may correspond with me by writing:

**Pamela Griffin**
**Author Relations**
**PO Box 719**
**Uhrichsville, OH 44683**

**ISBN 1-58660-921-1**

**HEART APPEARANCES**

*Our mission is to publish and distribute inspirational products offering exceptional value and biblical encouragements to the masses.*

All Scripture quotations are taken from the King James Version of the Bible.

All of the characters and events in this book are fictitious. Any resemblance to actual persons, living or dead, or to actual events is purely coincidental.

PRINTED IN THE U.S.A.

# one

## 1919

Darcy Evans was having a bad day. What's more, she certainly didn't need the added nuisance of a meddlesome porter hovering at her heels. Hugging her battered satchel, which contained the one spare dress the reformatory allowed upon her dismissal—all she had in the world—she turned and eyed the man suspiciously.

"Can I take that for you, Miss?" The hefty porter raised shaggy eyebrows and held out his huge calloused hand.

"No." Her reply was stiff, to the point. Why couldn't he leave her alone? He'd been watching her since she stepped off the train at Ithaca and began pacing the platform.

The porter tipped his cap and moved away. Darcy sighed with relief and scanned the area with expectancy. The afternoon sun edged the trees and surrounding buildings with harsh white light, and the burnt-coal smell from the smokestack lingered in the damp air. Black specks of cinder from the departed train still floated through the sky, though she'd been waiting on this platform for what seemed an eternity.

*Oh, pigeon feathers!* Had Charleigh really forgotten her? What other explanation could there be for her not meeting the train?

A slight smile tipped Darcy's mouth as she thought of her redheaded friend. When Darcy first met Charleigh in a holding cell in England, she was confused, to say the least. To discover Charleigh had turned herself in to Scotland Yard went against every survival tactic Darcy had been taught by Hunstable and Crackers—two childhood accomplices who'd shown her all she needed to know about surviving on the streets of London.

Charleigh had exhibited a strange peace, a calm relief—as though she were actually happy to pay for her crimes. Something about the secretive woman had drawn Darcy, like a starved cat to a cooked leg of pheasant. At first she'd been a little put off by Charleigh's talk of Jesus and salvation; but after two years at Turreney Farm, Darcy saw something in Charleigh she'd seen in no one else. A peaceable attitude. A glow in her eyes. A knowledge that God loved her—no matter what. And Darcy wanted what she'd seen.

Still, after Charleigh's sentence was over—three months before Darcy's—it had been easy for Darcy to slip back into the old life. All too soon she found herself back in the reformatory, serving a second sentence for drunkenness and petty theft. Near the end of her term, the barrister who'd represented Charleigh arrived with a letter expressing her desire to have Darcy come to Lyons's Refuge—the reformatory for boys that Charleigh's husband had founded in upstate New York—and help there. Darcy had readily agreed. There had been a lot of what the barrister called "legal matters" to wade through, but soon Darcy found herself on a steamer headed for America.

And now here she was, after coming all this way and traveling for five days, with no one here to greet her.

Frustrated, Darcy plopped down on the wooden bench along the station wall and slapped her hand to the crown of her floppy black hat.

Had Charleigh really forgotten her?

ও

Grimacing, Brent Thomas picked up the mesh sack from the driver's seat with his thumb and forefinger. He marched over the damp ground with the odorous parcel and flung it into the nearby field, wishing he knew which of his nine charges had thought it amusing to place a bag of dung on the wooden seat. He entertained a fairly good idea of the culprit's identity but wasn't certain. Furthermore, he couldn't discipline every boy at the reformatory for one child's prank, though he knew his mentor would have had no compunction in doing so. Professor

Gladsbury was a stern instructor, and though Brent had appreciated the elderly man's wisdom, he'd never agreed with his strict methods of discipline, such as the harsh raps on the palm with a willow stick. And yet, on days like today. . .

"Brent! Wait!"

Mrs. Lyons's shout halted him as he finished wiping off the seat. He turned to watch the headmaster's British wife hurry down the three porch steps, waving an envelope in her hand.

Brent was already late for the station, having had to change into his one spare pair of trousers after his encounter with the reeking bag. Absentmindedness often made him act without being aware of his surroundings—seating himself without looking, for instance. Something the culprit was sure to know.

He offered a penitent smile. "I'm terribly sorry, Mrs. Lyons, I realize I'm late to collect your friend. Would you like me to post that while I'm in town?"

She brushed a fiery lock of hair from her face. "Yes, please," she said after she'd caught her breath and handed him the envelope. "Now, do remember, Brent. Darcy's been through a great deal, so she might not be quite—shall we say, personable, at first. But Stewart and I have prayed, and we feel God wants her here at the Refuge. That's why we've done everything to make such an occurrence possible, including sending money for her passage."

Brent nodded, uneasy. Why was she telling him this? He knew most of it. He wasn't certain he was altogether in favor of bringing an ex-felon to help out at a reformatory for young boys, but he trusted Stewart's judgment. Furthermore, Stewart's wife, being an ex-felon herself, was certainly a changed person from the woman she once described.

She grinned. "You're probably wondering why I'm sharing this with you. The truth is, well, you're a wonderful instructor to the boys and a rock of support when my husband is away. Stewart and I know we can depend on you—with our very lives if need be. Why, I don't know what we would've done without you when Stewart went to France to fight in the war.

You've become more than a schoolteacher to us. You've become a friend. . . ."

Brent could feel the dreaded "but" coming.

"But, well, you're a trifle stuffy. And Darcy isn't the sort of person you're accustomed to."

Stuffy? She thought him stuffy? Just because he believed in dressing impeccably and using drawing room manners at all times? So, he did make sure everything went into its proper place. It didn't necessarily make him "stuffy." He removed his spectacles and cleaned them with the crisp handkerchief he'd placed in his pocket for that purpose.

"Oh dear," she murmured. "I've offended you, haven't I? I shouldn't have spoken. I simply wanted you to be prepared. Darcy isn't a woman with social graces—such as the women whose company you're accustomed to. That's the only reason I spoke—to prepare you. I never intended to injure your feelings."

"That's perfectly all right." He replaced his glasses and folded his handkerchief into thirds, tucking it back into his pocket.

"I wish I could go with you, but of course someone has to stay with the boys. Between Irma and me, we'll have our hands full."

He attempted a smile. "No explanations are necessary, Mrs. Lyons. I shall deliver your friend to you with all expedience." Still smarting from her comment, he added, "And I'm sure we'll get along splendidly."

❧

Darcy sat on the bench and kicked at the wooden planks with the toe of her scuffed shoe. Hunger gnawed at her insides. Remembering the brown paper bag of walnuts she'd bought at the wharf before boarding the train, she pulled the small sack from her valise. Setting a nut on the platform before her, she pulled up the frayed hem of her black skirt several inches and brought the heel of her shoe down hard on the shell.

With satisfaction, she heard the resulting *CRRRAAACKK* and bent to scoop her treat from the ground. She pulled the shell fragments away, popped the nutmeat into her mouth, and chewed with unabashed delight. Sensing someone watching, she turned her head sharply to the side.

A well-dressed young man stood nearby. He stared at her in horror, his blue eyes wide behind the wire-rimmed spectacles perched on his rather long nose. His light hair was combed neatly under a bowler hat, and a clean and pressed dark brown suit covered his slim form.

Darcy suddenly felt like a mangy cat next to this fancy-dressed bloke. Her woolen skirt was moth-eaten, her non-matching jacket was threadbare with ugly patches at the elbows, and she'd stuffed an old piece of cloth into the toe of one shoe to cover the hole as best she could. Her chin went up in defense. "Well, whatcha lookin' at, Guv'ner?"

He continued to gape, then slowly shook his head. "Excuse me, but you aren't Miss Evans, are you?" He sounded as though he believed he'd made a mistake, and he turned to go.

"Aye, that be me!" Darcy shot to her feet, tossing the shell remnants to the ground. She brushed the residue from her palms onto her skirt. " 'Ave you word on Charleigh? Is she comin' ter get me?"

He faced her again. Something like pained acceptance filled his eyes before he answered. "Not exactly. She sent me. I'm Brent Thomas, the schoolmaster at Lyons's Refuge."

Darcy gave a short nod and looked beyond him. Her eyes narrowed in suspicion. "Where's yer buggy? I don't see it."

"I had an errand to run. My wagon is on the other side, next to the post office." He let out a long, weary breath, shook his head, then closed the few steps between them and bent over, putting his hand to the handle of her bag. "If you'll follow me, Miss Evans—"

Darcy reacted quickly. She wrested the valise away from his grip, knocking him off balance. He fell against the bench with a surprised groan. Straightening, he rubbed his leg where it had made contact with the sharp corner of the bench and regarded her, his eyes wide in disbelief.

Darcy felt a momentary pang of guilt. "I like ter carry me own baggage," she explained. Head held high, she strode from the platform and turned the corner in what she hoped was the direction of the buggy.

❧

Brent stared after the tiny woman in rags, walking with the air of a queen. He shook his head. What had Stewart and Charleigh gotten themselves into? What had *he* gotten himself into?

Hurrying after the woman, Brent watched as she threw the valise onto the wagon seat. Grabbing both sides, she vaulted herself up next to the baggage in a most unladylike manner and flopped down. He briefly closed his eyes. Charleigh had tried to warn him, but he'd been too intent on her remark concerning his stuffiness to pay much heed.

"Guv'ner, hain't we goin'? I'm a mite 'ungry, I ham."

Brent winced. Her brutal attack on the English language was nothing short of criminal. The way she dropped h's and added h's where they weren't supposed to be thoroughly unsettled him. In addition, her vowels came out sounding like other vowels. It was a wonder he could understand a thing she said.

"Yes, I'm coming," he muttered, striding to the driver's side. Carefully he stepped up into the wagon and lowered himself onto the bench. With meticulous precision, he smoothed his suit coat and pants and adjusted his hat before grabbing the reins. Feeling her stare, he turned her way.

Her thin face wore an expression of humorous disbelief; both black brows arched high above her dark eyes.

"Something amuses you, Miss Evans?" Brent asked in a controlled voice. He guided the horses down the road leading to the lane that would take them to the reformatory.

"Nothin', Guv'ner. Nothin' ter squawk habout anyways."

Brent concentrated on the drive.

The minutes passed in blissful silence. Autumn had come in a blaze of glory, wrapping the trees in a cloak of fire. The sky held a grayish white cast, as luminescent as a pearl polished to a fine gleam. He felt a poem coming on and wished for his journal.

*CRRRAAAACKK!*

Startled by the explosive thud—which shook the wagon seat—Brent whipped his head toward Darcy. Bent at the waist, she retrieved something from under her boot. She straightened and looked at him. Seeing his horrified gaze upon her, she hesitated and then held out her hand. A mangled walnut lay in her dirty palm.

"Would ye loik some, Guv'ner?"

"No, thank you." Brent faced front again.

Social graces? The woman didn't know the meaning of the term. Furthermore, judging from what he'd seen of her character thus far, her housekeeping and culinary skills were likely nonexistent. He doubted she could read or write. So why had Charleigh wanted to bring her to the States so desperately?

A ghastly thought hit Brent, making him gasp as if someone had punched him in the stomach. Surely Stewart and Charleigh wouldn't do such a thing to him. No, Brent was only borrowing trouble, conjuring up all manner of ridiculous scenarios. Besides, nine small hooligans were enough for any schoolmaster to contend with.

*CRRRAAACCCKK!*

He braced himself against the wagon seat, closed his eyes, and sighed. It would be a long drive.

※

The wagon eventually neared a wooden fence. Darcy could see a wide field of grass beyond the slats and a large stone and wood house in the distance. She sat up straighter and craned her neck. A sign at the open gate welcomed her, and she struggled to make out the words. The first word—"Lyons's"— she recognized. It had been in the letter from Charleigh. The second word was harder, and she drew her brows together, sounding it out as Charleigh had taught her years ago.

Puzzled, she turned to the man beside her. "What's 'refug'?"

"What?" He glanced her way, incredulous, as if she'd just

asked him what color underdrawers he wore instead of the meaning of a simple word.

"Refug. What the sign says."

Brent sighed again. "That's refuge. Lyons's Refuge. The name of the reformatory."

"Oh." Darcy studied her new home.

A white picket fence enclosed vast grounds, where several horses grazed. Neat rows of vegetables grew on a small patch next to the two-story house. Dormer windows made the place look homier, and bright flowers spilled from window boxes in profusion. As she watched, a buxom red-haired woman opened the door and stepped onto the porch. Even from this distance, Darcy recognized her friend.

Before the wagon rolled to a stop, Darcy grabbed her bag with one hand, put her other to the back of her hat, and jumped to the ground, ignoring Brent's warning to wait. She raced across the wet grass to meet Charleigh coming down the steps. The two women hugged each other tightly.

"Oh, Charleigh, don't ye look grand!" Darcy exclaimed once she pulled away and eyed Charleigh's plump figure and rosy face. "Married life agrees with ye, hit does."

Charleigh smiled. "Now, let me look at you." She scanned Darcy's scarecrowlike form and frowned. "The reform still skimps on clothing allowances, I see. And meals."

"Hain't so bad," Darcy insisted. "Hat least I got me a spare dress. Some girls don't get that. Has for food, well. . .I ham a mite 'ungry."

Charleigh laughed. "Of course you are! Come along." She hooked her arm through Darcy's and led her to the porch. "Irma has prepared a special meal to welcome you. And about clothing, I have some dresses I can no longer wear. We can alter them to fit."

Darcy halted. "Charleigh! You're not—"

"No," Charleigh said, shaking her head. Pain filled her eyes, but she gave a wobbly half smile. "I was, but I lost the baby two months ago. And another at the beginning of the year."

"Oh, I ham sorry. I ought not ter 'ave said a thing."

"You didn't know." Charleigh squeezed Darcy's arm. "It's the one thing I wish I could give Stewart—a child. But maybe I never can." Her brow furrowed, a ghost of the past flitting across her face. Darcy had seen it often when they shared a room at Turreney Farm.

"Charleigh?" Darcy prodded softly.

Charleigh blinked, and a bright smile replaced the frown. "Just listen to me—all gloom and doom, and on your first day here! Come along, and let's see you fed."

ﾟ

Brent watched the women enter the house. Then, remembering the reason for his delay to the train station, he stepped down from the wagon and strode to the vegetable patch. Three boys knelt in dirt furrows, pulling up turnips under an older boy's watchful eye.

Herbert, a recent admission to Lyons's Refuge, flickered an uneasy glance at Brent. His freckled face reddened, and his gaze zoomed back to the vegetable in his hands as he slowly dropped it in the bucket beside him. He'd always been as easy to see through as a windowpane. His every action pointed to his guilt.

Joel dusted his hands on his trousers and met Brent's inquiring stare with a steady, questioning gaze. To a stranger, his angelic face, clear blue eyes, and halo of white blond hair would have labeled him an innocent. Yet Brent knew better. Joel was often the mastermind behind pranks. He could lie through his teeth without flinching, a convincing look on his face the entire time—confusing the questioner and making him feel at fault for even asking the boy if he was involved in any wrongdoing. That his father was a con artist serving time in prison came as no surprise.

And then there was Tommy. Brent inwardly sighed. Poor lad. A clubfoot disabled him, and he was wont to jump to another's suggestion of mischief in the hopes of being accepted by his peers. He swiped away a lock of mousy brown hair from his forehead and studied Brent with solemn dark eyes that held a world of pain. The boy had been thrown out by what was left of his family, scorned by many, and later found scavenging in the streets. Stealing the grocer's apples had been his first offense, but Stewart had taken pity on the lad when Judge Markham presented Tommy's case and had brought him to Lyons's Refuge more than a year ago.

"Boys, there's something I wish to discuss with you. Samuel, please unhitch Polly from the wagon and tend to her."

"Yes, Sir." Samuel, one of the original members of Lyons's Refuge, moved toward the horse, his expression curious in the eye not covered with the black patch. He'd come quite a ways from the boy who'd set fire to a farmer's field years ago. Upon coming home from fighting in the Great War, blinded in one eye from shrapnel, he'd sought a job at the Refuge and did whatever was needed of him.

Brent produced his most stern gaze as he assessed the three young culprits in his charge. "As to the matter of what I found on the wagon seat earlier—and I'm certain all three of you know to what I refer—I wish to know which one of you was responsible for leaving me that undesirable gift."

Herbert sniggered nervously. Joel affected his usual innocent pose. Tommy looked down at his hands.

Brent lifted an eyebrow, crossing his arms. "Very well. If none of you will admit to the crime, then all may suffer for it. I suspect the smaller boys didn't have a hand in this; but if I don't learn the truth soon, I'll be forced to inflict group punishment."

Tommy's glance shot upward, then dove to his hands again. "I did it, Mr. Thomas," he admitted in a low voice.

Joel gave him a look of disgust, Herbert one of surprise.

Brent doubted Tommy was the only boy involved; but before he could comment further, Irma called from the porch.

"Look lively, boys! Dinner's a-waitin'."

The three shot up from the ground at the cook's announcement, grabbed their pails, and scuttled like fleeing mice.

Tommy shuffled behind, trying to keep up.

"Stop where you are!" Brent's shout halted them in their tracks, and they turned, fidgety. "This conversation will resume after the meal. Is that understood?"

All three nodded, obviously relieved to have escaped judgment for however long it lasted. They tromped up the steps and disappeared through the doorway.

Shaking his head in frustration, Brent followed. If the past three hours were anything to go by, he would be better off returning to his room at the back of the schoolhouse and staying there for the remainder of the evening. Surely things couldn't get any worse.

The moment the thought crossed his mind, Brent released a humorless laugh. Then again, at Lyons's Refuge, anything was possible. And with the unpredictable Miss Darcy Evans afoot, Brent had an uneasy feeling the absurd would soon be considered the norm.

## two

The tantalizing aroma of roast beef and potatoes teased Brent's senses as he approached the dining table. Her face now free of soot, the newcomer sat next to Charleigh and stared ravenously at the platters of steaming food Irma set down. Brent took his usual seat, one catty-cornered across from Darcy, and she glanced at him.

He was struck by the intense midnight blue of her eyes—eyes so dark he'd thought the irises almost black earlier. But the electric lamps overhead revealed a trace of bluish purple in the dark orbs, something he hadn't noticed until now. Irritated that he *should* notice, Brent looked away, shook out his napkin, and placed it on his lap.

Once the boys were seated, with freshly scrubbed hands and faces, Charleigh bowed her head. "Merciful Lord, we thank You for this bounty. We ask You to bless everyone at this table, and thank You for granting safe passage to my friend, Darcy. We most humbly pray for Stewart's safe and speedy return to us from Manhattan. Amen."

A chorus of "amens" sounded. Clinks, scrapes, and muted thuds followed as helpings were scooped onto plates and platters, and dishes were passed among them.

"Tell us about your voyage, Darcy," Charleigh said from the head of the table. She spooned peas onto the plate of the youngest boy, Jimmy.

He screwed up his pixie face. "Don' want no peas."

"Hush," she admonished, "and eat them like a good lad." She turned her gaze Darcy's way. "Did you encounter any problems aboard ship?"

Darcy shook her head. "Nothin' 'appened—nothin' ter squawk habout, anyways," she said, her mouth full. "But it liked

16

to scare me witless when I 'eard a bang, and hit turned hout to be a clumsy crew member, what dropped a box o' books on deck!" She laughed with unsuppressed glee. "I thought some-one were takin' a shot hat us and the war 'ad started all over again."

Brent grimaced, carefully cut a bite-sized portion of meat, and slipped it into his mouth.

"Why does she talk so funny?" a boy said in a loud stage whisper to his peer. "And look at that ugly dress."

"We're not s'ppose to talk with our mouths full," young Jimmy informed Darcy with a superior air. "Mrs. Lyons says it ain't proper."

Brent looked up from his plate. Darcy appeared ill at ease as she fumbled with her glass of cider.

"Jimmy," Brent said, "children are also not supposed to cor-rect their elders. Or speak unless they've been spoken to."

"Yes, Sir." Jimmy bowed his head.

Brent looked Darcy's way. She studied him, clearly puzzled, creases in her milk white forehead. Uncomfortable, he looked away—to Charleigh.

A gleam of wonder lit her eyes as she looked back and forth between him and Darcy, a soft smile on her lips.

Brent focused on his plate, determined to keep his mind on his meal. Was it so unusual that he'd taken up for the poor guttersnipe? He'd always possessed something of a soft spot for the underdog. That was one reason he'd taken the job of schoolmaster to a bunch of misfits who'd each experienced short careers as a hooligan. The other reason had involved his brother Bill.

Darcy cleared her throat, and Brent looked up. She straight-ened in her chair, shoulders back, her chin lifted in a regal position. With as much dignity as Brent imagined she could muster, she spoke to the boy across from her and two seats down.

"Would you *pleeease* pass the Uncle Fred?"

Stunned silence met her startling request—followed by the

boys' raucous laughter. They collapsed over their plates, holding their sides as if they would burst.

"She wants to eat Uncle Fred!"

"Poor ole chap—wonder who he is?"

"Is she a cannibal too?"

"What's a 'cabinnal'?"

"Boys!" Charleigh stood and clinked her spoon against her glass, demanding attention. "If you can't behave like proper gentlemen, then you may march to your rooms and do without supper. Is that understood?"

They quieted, a muffled snort escaping now and then. Straightening in their seats, they again focused on dinner.

"That's better." Charleigh sank to her chair and replaced her napkin on her lap. She threw an apologetic look to Darcy, whose color rivaled that of the beets in the serving dish.

"I—I'm a mite tired," she mumbled. "Hit were a long journey. I'd loik to go to me room now."

"Of course. I'll have Irma send you up a tray." Charleigh's troubled gaze went to Brent. "Would you mind taking Darcy's bag to her room?"

Remembering the previous and painful incident at the station when he'd tried to assist with her valise, he turned a wary look Darcy's way. "If she'll allow it."

Darcy nodded, eyes downcast. "Hit's at the bottom o' the apples an' pears."

Brent stared, uncomprehending. "Apples and pears?"

"She means stairs," Charleigh explained.

"Well, why don't she just say so?" Joel demanded. "Is she loony?" His question led to more chortles from the boys.

"Joel, that's enough!" Charleigh leveled a steady gaze at the culprit. "Darcy speaks Cockney, a rhyming slang I also grew up with. It's popular in the East End of London. Uncle Fred is the term for bread. And as for your insolent remark, you may march to your room this minute, young man. In this house we don't use spiteful words to hurt another person's feelings."

Joel glared at Charleigh, then Darcy, but obediently rose

from the table and left. Darcy stood, tears making her huge eyes sparkle. "I really ought ter go lie down, Charleigh. No need sendin' a tray. I hain't as 'ungry as I thought."

Charleigh's expression was sympathetic. "Irma, if you'll watch the boys, I'll show Darcy to her room."

Frowning, Brent secured Darcy's bag and followed the women up the carpeted staircase. Life at Lyons's Refuge had indeed undergone a drastic change. And he had a sneaking suspicion it wasn't for the better.

‎‮‭ ‬

The next morning, a tap sounded on the door. "Darcy? May I come in?"

Darcy turned from brushing the tangles out of her thick dark hair. Morning sunlight streamed into the cozy attic room through the small, arched window, casting her in a golden pool of floating dust motes. "Aye—ye may."

Charleigh opened the door and smiled. "Did you sleep well? Is the room to your liking?" She moved to the iron bedstead and sank to the mattress. "Oh dear. It's dusty in here, isn't it? I do apologize. I thought the cleaning had been taken care of. I'll tend to it right away."

"It weren't bad. And I don't mind tendin' to me own room, to help any way I can."

Darcy twisted her body around on the chair so she could get a better look at her friend. Charleigh seemed upset, distracted; maybe she regretted bringing Darcy to America. Especially after what happened last night. "Did you want ter talk with me?"

Charleigh clasped her hands around one crossed knee. "Yes, Darcy, I did. There's really no easy way to say this, and I certainly don't want to hurt your feelings, but. . ." She trailed off.

Lifting her chin, Darcy prepared for the worst.

"After what happened at dinner last evening, I've come to the conclusion that certain measures must be taken in order for things to run smoothly here. Children can often be cruel without meaning to be. The boys at Lyons's Refuge can be cruel on purpose. Many of them are hard, bitter—coming from situations that would melt the hardest of hearts."

Darcy nodded. Having come from just such a situation, she understood completely.

"First and foremost, I want you to know that I love you as you are." Charleigh smiled. "But in order to be understood— as well as to understand—I think it beneficial that you learn the proper way to talk here in America."

Darcy wrinkled her brow, uncertain if she should feel slighted, hurt, or relieved. Her manner of speech had never been a problem, though at the reform she'd been forced to drop the popular Cockney phrases. Nervousness at being in a new place had probably led her to say them without thinking last night. Ever since she'd arrived in the States, she'd felt buffeted by the peculiar yet precise way these Americans spoke. Even Charleigh's British accent was polished, like the high gloss of an apple—whereas Darcy's was as rough as a potato just dug from the earth.

Charleigh leaned forward, covering Darcy's hand with her own. "Darcy, if it was just me, I'd never suggest it. Yet, not only the boys, but also the whole town, will look at you askance. I've discovered that people often judge harshly what they don't understand, and I don't want you hurt. I want you to feel comfortable here. This is your home now."

Darcy gave a slight nod.

Charleigh's smile grew wide. "I'll help you with manners and deportment, as well as correct you when you use slang and the wrong pronunciation of words. I'd also like you to further your education in reading and writing. There's nothing wrong with increasing one's head knowledge."

At this, Darcy's heart lightened. She'd always wanted to read books, dreamed of it, wished she could flip through the pages with ease as Charleigh had always done. But Darcy could barely stumble over a paragraph. The little time Charleigh ferreted from daily chores to teach her at the women's reformatory hadn't been enough.

"Are ye certain you'll 'ave the time, Charleigh? Seems like an awful lot you're tykin' on, what with running the reform and tykin' care o' the boys."

Charleigh rose and averted her eyes, smoothing the wrinkles from her skirt. "Actually, Brent would be much better qualified to teach you. I'll suggest he tutor you for an hour every day once the children finish their lessons."

Darcy drew a soft breath. Brent Thomas teach her? She didn't think she could abide him looking down his nose at her day after day in confined quarters—and alone yet. True, he'd rescued her from total humiliation at dinner last night, but the blue eyes behind the spectacles had been full of pity. And Darcy wanted no man's pity! Yet she did want to learn all she could about reading and writing.

"Can I tyke the class wi' the others?" Darcy asked.

"After last night, I'm not sure that would be wise."

"I'd like ter give it a try. And Charleigh—I don't want to be a burden. Maybe Cook wouldn't mind 'aving me 'elp? I learned to bake some hat the farm after ye left."

"Yes—that would be splendid. I'm sure Irma would welcome any help. As to the other. . ." Charleigh pursed her lips in thought, then nodded once. "I'll discuss your request with Brent and see what he says."

❧

Brent stared at Charleigh, his forearms resting at either side of the open book on his desk. Certainly he hadn't heard her correctly. It had been a long morning. Fatigue must be clouding his mind.

"Well, Brent? Will you do it?"

The screeching sound of chalk on slate made him wince. He looked across the room toward the offender, who was writing for the twenty-second time, "I will never again place bags of horse manure on wagon seats or any other vehicle. But I will leave the manure in the field where it belongs."

"Tommy, you may go for now," Brent said. "You can resume the one hundred sentences later this afternoon."

"Thank you, Mr. Thomas." Relief sweeping his features, the boy set down the chalk and limped from the room.

Brent turned his gaze to Charleigh, who stood in front of his desk. He adjusted his spectacles with thumb and forefinger. "Now let me see if I understand you correctly, Mrs. Lyons. You wish for me to train your friend in the rudiments of grammar, reading, and penmanship by allowing her to attend my class?"

Charleigh beamed. "Yes, that's right."

Brent held back a groan. "Judging from last night's fiasco, are you certain that would be wise? Maintaining order in this classroom is often a delusion. Don't you think bringing in a young woman—who obviously is far below the boys academically—would only create further problems at best? At worst, total chaos?"

"Darcy assures me that she would feel more comfortable in a classroom environment. All I ask is that we give this a try. If it doesn't work, then of course we'll arrange an alternative method."

What alternative method Charleigh had in mind, Brent didn't want to know; though he could hazard a guess.

Charleigh shifted her weight to her other foot. "Please, Brent. Darcy is special to me. She has been ever since I met her in a holding cell in London. From then on, every day with her endeared her to me all the more. I want to help her by seeing to it she receives the education she needs to coexist with the townspeople, as well as those here at the Refuge."

Brent pondered her words, his hand reaching for a nearby fountain pen and repeatedly tapping first one end, then the other, on the desk. Charleigh's husband had been there for Brent when he was fresh out of college, full of hopes and dreams. His brother's criminal activities became known not two months after Brent graduated—a horrible shock to the entire family. Because of Bill's folly, Brent was denied every position he applied for that summer. Only Stewart had entrusted him with his first teaching position—ironically at a boys' reformatory. Only Stewart had shown faith in him when others had snubbed him.

Brent thought about Darcy at dinner last night. Something about the little wren twisted his heart, though he was loath to admit it. Would this one good deed be such a difficult task?

He let the air escape his lungs and set down the pen. "Very well, Mrs. Lyons. You may tell Miss Evans that I'll expect her in my classroom tomorrow morning at eight."

Charleigh gave him a brilliant smile. "Thank you! I'm certain you won't regret it."

Brent watched her hurry out the door as though afraid he might change his mind. A picture of the vivacious and impulsive Darcy Evans suddenly invaded his thoughts, and he closed his eyes.

Regret it? He already did.

ખ

Ten minutes before class was to start, Darcy nervously tramped to the small, shingled building set off from the main house. Inside, desks sat in three neat rows. A huge chalkboard stood beside the schoolmaster's desk, with a shelf of chunky books along the wall behind it. The only source of light came from a window near the teacher—and the few lamps bracketed to the board walls. In the corner, an ancient-looking potbellied stove gave off welcome heat.

" 'Ello!" Darcy directed an uncertain smile at Brent. He looked up from his desk, gave a vague nod, then turned back to writing something in a thin book.

The smile slipped from her face. She may not be the queen, but didn't she deserve some type of common courtesy? A hello in return? Or a polite "Good morning"?

"Whatcha doin', Guv'ner? Today's lesson?"

"No," he muttered, his gaze never straying from the book.

When nothing else was offered, she sighed and scanned the desks. "Where ham I ta sit then?"

"Wherever you like," he returned, his gaze still plastered to that book.

Blowing out her breath in a loud burst of frustration, Darcy plopped onto the nearest bench and tried to squeeze her legs underneath. The desk was much too low and settled on her skirt. Drawing her brows together, she swung her legs out to the right, then settled her elbows on the desk—but now her body was twisted sideways. This would never do!

"Guv'ner?"

He sighed. "What now?"

She crossed her arms on the desk and glared at him. "I don't see 'ow I'm to learn to write good hif I 'ave to stoop like an ole woman to do it!"

"What?"

To her satisfaction, he raised his head, looking startled. He eyed the table where it hit below her waist. His brows gathered. "I'd forgotten about that. The desks were custom-made by one of the locals. He fashioned them for small boys."

Her chin lifted. "Which I hain't."

"Which I'm not."

Her brow creased in confusion. "What?"

"Which I'm not. If I'm to teach you proper grammar, we may as well begin now."

"An' what about the desk, Guv'ner?"

With a sigh, he slammed his book shut. "I suppose, until we find something more suitable, you'll have to move up here with me."

If he'd asked her to parade around the room in her bloomers, she couldn't have been more shocked. "With you?"

He tilted his head. "Unless you have a better idea? My desk seems to be the only one that's the right height. And, as you've pointed out, it's important to maintain correct posture when learning penmanship. Take that chair in the corner. The boys should be along any minute." He began moving stacks of books off one edge of his desk and onto the floor.

Darcy hesitated, then went to retrieve the chair. Noisily, she dragged it across the planks, set it in position, walked to the front of it, and plopped down again. "All right. Now what?"

He looked away from sorting a stack of books and adjusted his spectacles. Sunlight pouring in from the window made the curling edges of his still-damp hair glisten. Up close, his eyes were bluer than she remembered, and the fact that she noticed made her fidget.

"I suppose we should see just how far along you are academically before the rest of the class arrives."

"A–ca–dem. . . ?"

"In your schooling." He set a slate in front of her and slapped a piece of chalk on top. "Write your letters, if you please."

Darcy could do that. She had used a pointed stick in the reform's garden and scratched letters into the dirt while Charleigh watched. Eagerly, Darcy picked up the chalk and began forming each letter, sucking in her lower lip in concentration. She ran out of space when she still had five more to go and turned the slate so she could squeeze some along the edge, then turned it again to print upside down along the top.

"Finished!" she exclaimed, triumphant.

Brent turned from sorting the books to look. His eyebrows lifted. "Hmm. Next time don't make your letters so large, and you won't run out of room. Overall, it's adequate, I suppose."

She frowned and looked at the slate. Adequate? What did that mean? It didn't sound good.

"Now, let's hear you read." He opened a book to the first page and slid it in front of her.

Darcy hunched over, brow furrowed, and studied the black print. "A Boy's. . .Will. . .by. . ." Her brows bunched further. "Row-burt. . .Frost." She lifted her gaze to his, expecting praise for her success.

"That's Robert Frost," he said, closing the book. "With a short O. All right, that'll do for now."

That'll do? Darcy frowned. "So, ham I to learn from that book?"

"Hmm?" He looked up from jotting something down in another book. "Oh, yes, I see what you mean. Perhaps it's not suitable for a young woman. I hadn't thought of that. I'll look into acquiring more adequate literature for your schooling."

Adequate. There was that word again. Darcy had a feeling she would grow to despise it.

A flock of young boys burst through the schoolroom door, as noisy as a gaggle of geese. Their chattering and guffaws ceased when they saw Darcy.

"What's she doin' here?" the one Darcy remembered as Joel said. He frowned at her, probably blaming her for his being sent to his room without supper.

"Is she gonna teach us?" the smallest boy, Jimmy, piped up. "Is that why she's sitting at your desk, Mr. Thomas?"

"Ha! Her teach us? She can't even talk right."

"Then why's she here?"

Pulling the cap off his white blond hair, Joel let out a spiteful laugh. "I'll bet I can guess why she's sitting at his desk, all right. She's Teacher's new pet." He elbowed a gangly dark-haired boy next to him. "An' you know what that means with the likes o' her, don't ya? Smoochin' in the cloakroom, I reckon. Don't ya think so, Ralph?"

The dark-haired boy chuckled. Heat raced to Darcy's face as a few nervous titters filtered through the room.

"That will be enough!" Brent stood and rapped his ruler sharply on the edge of the desk, then snapped his forbidding gaze to Joel. "For your impertinence, Mr. Lakely, you may come an hour early to the classroom every day for the rest of this month and start the fire in the stove."

Joel's mouth tightened. "Yes, Sir."

Brent released a weary breath and set the ruler down. "Nor will I have any slang in this classroom."

"Yes, Sir."

"And you may apologize to Miss Evans."

"Wha—" At the teacher's lifted brow, Joel cut short his indignant reply. "Yes, Sir. Sorry, Miss Evans," he clipped, his eyes glittering with hate as he looked her way.

Brent sank back to his chair. "As to the numerous inquiries regarding Miss Evans's appearance in our classroom, she is to learn alongside you gentlemen. And I trust you *will* behave like gentlemen?"

Grumbles and groans met his query. Darcy gazed over the room of scrubbed faces, some curious, some suspicious, a few of them openly hostile, until she found a pair of kind brown eyes underneath a long swatch of mousy brown hair. The boy offered her a tentative smile. Darcy returned it. Perhaps things would soon improve.

"Pull out your slates and we'll begin today's lesson." Brent adjusted his glasses.

Darcy reached for the slate but in her haste knocked it off the desk. It hit the planked floor with a resounding clatter, eliciting another round of chortles from the boys. Her gaze whipped to Brent's weary one.

Then again, perhaps not.

# three

A streak of branched lightning zipped across the nighttime sky, making an erratic slash beyond the thicket at the eastern side of the house. Soon, a distant crash followed. Brent stood on the covered porch and listened to the rain beat down on an overturned barrel, similar to the sound of many drums. From behind, a muted yellow light shone on the porch. He turned to see who had joined him.

Looming over Brent by almost a foot, Stewart Lyons, the headmaster of Lyons's Refuge, came through the door. Premature gray sprinkled his hair, but his strapping build was that of a youth's. His hazel eyes lifted to the sky. "It looks as if the storm is passing."

Brent nodded. "It would appear so."

The light vanished as Stewart closed the door behind him. "That Darcy is something else. Imagine her saying that my fiddle playing reminded her of a rummy's who used to play at the tavern. She's certainly not afraid to speak her mind, is she?" Amusement laced his words.

"No, she's not." Brent returned his gaze to the rain. In the past weeks since he'd taken on the task of schooling her, he never knew what she would suddenly say or do next.

"Your situation reminds me of a play an acquaintance of mine attended years ago."

Brent winced. *Don't say it.*

"*Pygmalion,* I think it was called. Ever hear of it?"

Brent closed his eyes, resigned to his fate. "I remember reading the review. It's a play by Bernard Shaw, set in London, about a Cockney flower girl and a professor of diction."

"That's right. Though you hardly remind me of the irascible

28

Henry Higgins—at least from the way my friend described him." Stewart grinned.

Brent managed a smile. Well, that was a relief. Or was it in the same league as being considered stuffy?

The two men continued to stare at the storm, watching the lightning move northeast. When Stewart again spoke, Brent detected a somber tone in his voice. The trickling sound of rain falling from the eaves added to the dreary mood.

"I received a letter from my family in Raleigh today. My father is ill. It sounds serious."

"I'm sorry to hear that." Brent studied Stewart, whose hands were now shoved into his pockets. He looked more tense than usual, still staring into the dissipating storm.

"Thank you." Stewart glanced his way. "I'd like you to take my place while I'm gone—if I go. I haven't made a solid decision yet. I wanted to talk to you first. If it became known that three women were running the reform—two of them former felons and one an old woman—the state might take the boys. Judge Markham already considers our methods of reform unconventional. It took a great deal of persistence on my part to get his support when I first got started. Especially since the idea of reformatories was still so new and my concept was so unlike the others."

"If you do go, how long will you be gone?"

"I have no idea. My parents and I were never close, one reason I came to New York with my cousin, Steven. After his suicide, my family turned against me. But that's all history now." He sighed. "With Father ill and likely to die, I feel I've no option but to go to them. It's my duty. My oldest brother died in the war, and I'm the only son left." Stewart's words trailed off. "So many good men died. So many."

Uncomfortable, Brent looked away. Stewart never talked about the fighting he'd seen, and Brent preferred it that way. He settled his hat more firmly on his head. "I should return to my room. I have papers to grade."

"And about what I asked—would you be open to taking on

the job of temporary headmaster, as you did during the war?"

Brent nodded. "Of course. You can depend on me."

"Thank you, Friend. You're a good man."

Brent moved toward the schoolhouse and released a self-derisive laugh. A good man? Hardly. If the truth were known, he was a coward. When the Great War had been in progress, the prospect of fighting terrified him. Guns and grenades were not for him.

All through childhood, Brent's peers had labeled him "lily-livered." An appropriate title, to be sure. He lacked the bravado that made men like Stewart, who'd won a medal for saving his company of men, a hero in people's eyes. Moreover, it hadn't boosted Brent's self-esteem when, after being drafted, he was rejected for having flat feet. Even a plausible excuse for being unable to fight didn't erase the belief Brent fostered that had he been accepted, he would have abandoned his company in the heat of battle and fled. Like a lily-livered fool.

Unlike Stewart. The town's war hero.

❧

Darcy wiggled her back against the plump cushion, enjoying the fire's warmth. The boys sat in a semicircle on the rose-patterned carpet around Charleigh, who sat in a rocker, reading from a book. Nine pairs of eyes watched Charleigh's face as she brought Louisa May Alcott's words to life: " 'You cannot be too careful; watch your tongue, and eyes, and hands, for it's easy to tell, and look, and act untruth.' "

Darcy hid a smile at the rapt expressions on the boys' faces. Four weeks ago, when Charleigh first started reading *Little Men*, she'd been met with groans and complaints that it was a "sissified book." She ignored their objections and each Sunday evening read one chapter aloud. Soon the little scamps sat entranced, eyes shining, eagerly waiting to hear the latest goings-on at Plumcrest—the school that was as odd as Lyons's Refuge and also contained a variety of boys, some with quirks much like theirs. Darcy overheard the lads talk one night and knew that each identified with a certain boy in the story, and each looked forward to hearing what his character was up to next.

Darcy's gaze swept the nine upturned faces. A hint of innocence glimmered, even in the older ones' eyes. These boys were just boys, after all. Not miniature hooligans, as some of the townspeople whispered. Many of these lads had been dealt a hard lot in life and had done what they could to survive. How well Darcy understood them.

When Charleigh first explained how she and Stewart ran the place—by discipline mixed with love—Darcy had been perplexed. She'd been sentenced to only one reformatory—and that one for women. But the strict matrons, daunting schedules, and never-ending work could not equate with life at Lyons's Refuge. Here, Charleigh and Stewart treated the boys as if they were their own, though strict discipline was administered to those who didn't abide by the rules. In the two months since Darcy had arrived, she saw Lyons's Refuge more as a home for boys than a true reformatory.

Daily schedules included chores, schooling, and then more work around the farm. Filling meals cooked by Irma and Darcy satisfied the boys, who later would gather for thirty-minute devotions with Charleigh and Stewart, then hurry off to an hour of studying lessons before bedtime. Saturdays were much the same, with the exception of no classes, which gave more time to finish lessons Brent had assigned. And Sundays were days of rest at Lyons's Refuge.

Up early, Stewart and Charleigh took the three youngest boys to the country church a few miles away in Stewart's noisy motorcar, while Brent and Darcy took the rest in the wagon. Afterward they returned home to another sumptuous meal, and the boys were allowed a couple of hours' free time to do pretty much as they pleased. Before bed, Charleigh sat in the rocker by the fire, with the boys gathered around, and read them a chapter from God's Holy Word. She then picked up a book—sometimes Charles Dickens or Robert Louis Stevenson or another author's work. But always it was a story to fuel every boy's imagination and make each face glow with anticipation.

The front door opened, letting in a blast of cold, snowy air; and Darcy looked toward the foyer. Brent walked in, his spectacles immediately fogging from the warm room. His bowler hat, scarf, and coat were speckled with white. He pulled off his glasses and glanced at Charleigh, whose back was to him, then at Darcy. Putting a finger to his lips, he shook his head, then quietly moved to the back of the house.

Darcy hesitated for two full paragraphs of the story before rising and going in search of him. The others didn't notice her leave; or if they did, they paid no attention.

She found Brent in the kitchen, pulling the loaf of bread from the bread box. He turned upon hearing her footsteps.

"Hello," Darcy said, remembering to pronounce her "H" as Charleigh had taught her. "We missed you at dinner."

He gave a slight nod. "I had grades to average. The time slipped by me unawares." With a knife, he sawed two pieces from the rye loaf and set them at precise angles on a plate.

Darcy noticed he wasn't wearing his spectacles. Without them, his eyes appeared much bluer and brighter. Flustered that she should pick up on such a thing, she looked away, to the table. His glasses lay on top.

Not thinking, Darcy plucked them up. She raised them to the light, peered through the fogged lenses, rubbed them on her skirt, and, curiosity getting the best of her, slipped them on.

"Aaeee!" she squealed. "Things appear as they did years ago—when I was about in me cups!"

Heat rushed to her face when she realized what she'd blurted. Though she'd learned much about manners since coming to Lyons's Refuge, too often the past slipped out to embarrass her.

Brent said nothing. After a moment he cleared his throat and lifted the spectacles from Darcy's nose. "Yes, well, they aid me in my vision impairment."

She watched as he slipped them back on. He looked at her for a few seconds before turning to butter his bread.

"I have some stew in the icebox for you," Darcy said. She opened the one door of the tin-lined wooden contraption where Irma stored perishable food. Blocks of ice kept the interior cold. "I'll heat it on the stove and dish you up a bowl."

"No, really, the bread is enough."

"It won't be no bother," Darcy insisted, pulling the container off the shelf and slamming the door shut.

"Really, Miss Evans, there's no need—"

Darcy swung around and crashed into Brent, who'd come up behind her. The uncovered beef stew splashed onto his pristine linen shirt and tweed vest. Involuntarily, Darcy dropped the pan, her hands flying to her mouth in horror. The pan hit the floor, splashing the wooden planks, her skirt, and Brent's neat, creased pants with the rest of the brown juice.

Darcy's shocked gaze flew to Brent's. His eyes were filled with what looked like pained acceptance—something she'd seen many times. He moved his once-shiny brown shoe to dislodge a potato slice that rested on top.

"Perhaps I'll forgo dinner tonight. I'm really not as hungry as I thought." His smile was feeble at best.

"I—I'm sorry," Darcy stuttered, backing up. "Really, I ham." Slowly she shook her head, then hurried from the room.

&

Brent watched her go, his mind a tangle of thoughts that resembled Charleigh's wild ivy growing on the windowsill. Perhaps he shouldn't have said what he had. With a heavy sigh, he reached for the dish towel, dampened it with water from the pump, and blotted his clothes, attempting to remove the stains.

Darcy remained an enigma. One minute she was bold and brassy, saying whatever she pleased; the next she was as sensitive as a child whose pencil drawing had been ridiculed by an unfeeling adult. Brent was frankly astounded at her intelligence and at how quickly she learned. She wasn't far from catching up to the boys in her studies. Grammatically and in areas of deportment, Charleigh had worked wonders with her.

Though, of course, the young Miss Evans still had a great deal to learn.

Brent never knew what to expect from the British spitfire. She was a cyclone in his well-ordered and perfectly planned existence. A cyclone that tore from the roots everything proper, staid, and orderly, in Brent's estimation, and replaced it with impulsiveness, disorder—and a zest for living and having fun.

He glanced at the spill on the floor and bent to mop it up with the dishcloth. He'd never experienced fun or even been allowed to play. His parents had raised him with a rigid code of conduct—so severe that it sent his brother running from home before his sixteenth birthday. Brent shook his head, sobering at the thought of Bill and the life of crime he'd chosen. Bill and he had been so close once. . . .

Releasing a forceful breath, and with it any bitter thoughts of what might have been, Brent rinsed out the towel and laid it over the rack by the counter. He shrugged into his outerwear and left by the back door.

# four

With unabashed delight, Darcy crunched into her apple. Her eyelids slid shut. "Mmmmm. . .I think apples is—are—my favorite fruit of all. Next to oranges an' pears. An' maybe plums."

"Didn't you like them pies, Miss Darcy?" young Jimmy asked.

"Well, the mincemeat pie we had for Thanksgiving sure was good, it was; but I think the fruitcake we ate earlier today topped 'em all."

"I like oranges best," Tommy said as he limped to her chair near the Christmas tree.

She put her arm around him, bringing him close. Tommy was Darcy's favorite of the boys, reminding her of Roger, a lame child who'd been in her young band of thieves. As she'd done with Roger, Darcy took Tommy under her wing.

He pulled a shiny silver whistle out of the darned sock he held, then tipped it over to let several jacks and a ball fall into his palm. "Isn't this just the greatest, Miss Darcy? Mrs. Lyons's pop sure is a nifty guy. I never had no toys gived to me before I come to this place."

"Yes, he is a nifty guy," Darcy agreed, remembering her first meeting with Michael Larkin and his wife, Alice. He accepted her immediately, despite her way of talking; and Darcy soon realized the Irish bear of a man had a heart as gentle as a cub's. A huge contributor to the reform, Michael visited often, seeming to adopt the boys as his grandsons.

Darcy looked past the tall green fir—decorated with stringed popcorn, cutout cookies, and colorful paper chains the boys had made—to where Charleigh sat beside her father on the sofa. Stewart stood nearby, his back to them, and stared out the window at the falling snow. Charleigh and her father were in deep discussion; and from the looks of it, the topic was serious. Charleigh shook her head in reply to something Michael said. He patted her hand; and she swiped a finger underneath her eye, pasted on a smile, and stood. "Well, boys. What say we have some gingerbread and hot cocoa to end this Christmas Day?"

Loud cheers and whoops met her suggestion.

She put up her hands for quiet, then turned to Darcy. "But first I'd like you to read the Christmas story. Every year we take turns. Since this is your first year with us, I'd like you to do the honors."

The juice from the apple seemed to evaporate in Darcy's mouth, which went stone dry. "Me?" With difficulty she swallowed the chewed bite. "Maybe Mr. Thomas should read instead." She cast a hopeful glance at Brent.

"Please, Darcy," Charleigh insisted. "You've come so far in your education since the day you arrived. I'd love to hear you read." Her gaze encompassed the children scattered on the floor. "Wouldn't we, boys?"

A chorus of mumbled agreements filled the room.

From beside the fireplace, Joel blew his new whistle, catching everyone's shocked attention. His smile was wide. "Aw, Mrs. Lyons, don't make her read if she can't do it." His clear blue eyes held a smirk as they turned Darcy's way. "I mean, we don't want to embarrass her or nothin'—like when she read aloud from *Paradicee Losit* her first week at school. Or at least that's how she said it."

"Joel." Stewart turned from the window, giving the boy a warning look. "Hold your tongue."

Darcy's lips thinned at the unwanted memory; and she glared at the scamp, who sat on the carpet, legs crossed, and stared innocently back. She turned her gaze to Charleigh and held out her hand. "Give me the book." She'd show the little rapscallion.

With an encouraging smile, Charleigh handed her the

Bible, showed her the passage, and rejoined her father on the couch. Darcy took a deep breath and briefly closed her eyes, delivering a hasty, silent prayer that she wouldn't get any of the words wrong.

" 'And it came to pass in those days, that there went out a de-cree from Cae-sar Aug-us-tus, that all the world should be. . .taxed. . .' "

She continued to read, sounding out the longer words. But she was certain she didn't mispronounce a single one. The simple yet fascinating story of Christ's birth produced an awed hush in the room, despite the halting manner in which the events were told. Even Darcy felt a sweet peace as she read the words, " 'Fear not: for, be-hold, I bring you good ti-dings of great joy, which shall be to all people. For unto you is born this day in the city of David a Sa-viour, which is Christ the Lord. . .' " Darcy paused for a moment. "And sud-den-ly there was with the angel a mul-ti-tude of the heav-en-ly host praising God, and saying, Glory to God in the highest, and on earth peace, good will toward men.' "

She looked up from the book. No animosity or mockery shone from Joel's eyes now. They were soft and wondering, like a child's. Sometimes it was hard to remember he *was* only a child. And suddenly Darcy knew she would do what she could to help the boy escape a life such as hers had been. How to go about such a task was the mystery. For surely trying to help such a stubborn lad would be a chore more taxing than any duties she'd had at Turreney Farm or the cooking she did at the Refuge.

Irma cleared her throat. "I never get weary of hearing that story, and it seems I hear something different with each tellin' of the tale." Wiping her eyes with the edge of her apron, she turned in the direction of the kitchen, then stopped and faced them, her gaze sweeping over the room. "Well, what are you just sitting there and staring for? Look lively, laddies! Hot cocoa's awaitin'."

Her reply had the effect of a trumpet at reveille. The boys

clambered to their feet, whistles and jacks forgotten, and shot toward the kitchen. Even Stewart's remonstration to "hold it down" seemed softer than usual. He moved across the room and took hold of his wife's hand, helping her from the sofa.

Charleigh cast a glance Darcy's way. "Coming, Darcy? I can try to save you a cup, but with that crowd, I can't offer any promises."

Darcy shook her head. With one hand, she closed the Bible and set it on the piecrust table beside her. "Apples is enough for me. I prefer fruit and nuts and the like."

Charleigh smiled and left the room with Stewart, and Michael and Alice followed.

❧

"Aren't you going to join the party?" Darcy asked Brent when they were the only ones left in the parlor.

He shook his head. "I've never had a penchant for such festivities."

She propped her elbow on the chair arm and rested her chin on her palm, studying him where he sat in a stiff-backed chair. "Not sure what a 'penchant' is, but if it means you don't like to have fun, why not?"

"Excuse me?" Brent lifted his eyebrows in astonishment.

"Fun. F—u—n. Fun." She threw him a wicked smile. "See, I can spell it too. But spelling don't—doesn't—do me much good if I can't live it. Just spelling words and reading 'em don't do much of anything. You got to live 'em too."

Baffled, he merely shook his head.

Darcy leaned forward, tucking her wrists in her skirt between her knees, her half-eaten apple still in one hand. "I'll bet you're wonderin' how a girl like me could have had any fun in her life."

"The thought had crossed my mind," Brent admitted. "Lyons's Refuge is in a class by itself, it's true, but I know most reforms are quite strict."

"See there!" She rolled her eyes as if he wore a dunce cap. "You got to tyke what fun you can find in life when you can find it. Now at the women's reform it was harder, I'll admit, and things wasn't one bit pleasant. Just ask Charleigh; she'll tell you. I learned to look for fun in the small things—like when I was hoein' the vegetable patch, and a butterfly would flutter past me face. I'd watch it and imagine I was ridin' on its back, seein' everything it saw beyond the gates of the reform. Do you know what I'm sayin'?"

Brent nodded, though he had no idea what she was talking about.

"When I was with Hunstable and Crackers—they was two of the gang, a few years older than I and smart as the dickens— they taught me how to have fun. Especially Crackers, our leader. He could pick any pocket and had a fondness for crackers. That's why we called him Crackers. He stole 'em from the grocer's barrel. Practically lived on 'em, he did!" She laughed.

"I hardly see how thievery could be classified as fun. You've seen what wages it brings."

"No, that's not the fun I was talking about," Darcy said and sighed, shaking her head in exasperation. "I'm gettin' to that. Stealin' was the same as survivin' in the East End, 'specially if you was a child. Me mum died when I was young, and me stepfather—well, let's just say he weren't a nice man. He'd get drunk and come after me. One day I had enough. I ran out and never went back. I was ten at the time. That's when I joined up with Crackers and Hunstable. They found me sleepin' in the street under a newspaper." She shrugged one shoulder, crunched another bite of her apple, and smiled as though the event hadn't been of any real concern to her.

Brent stared, uncertain how to reply. This was the first time he'd been given a glimpse into Darcy's past. Though his childhood could never be called easy, his physical comforts had been met. He was stunned at the hardships some children endured. Children such as Charleigh and Darcy had been, and the boys at Lyons's Refuge.

"Tell me about Crackers's idea of fun," he said softly.

She cocked a surprised brow and peered at him as if trying

to discern whether he was truly interested, then gave a nod and swallowed her apple. "There was this organ grinder, see, and he had this monkey—it wore a red satin jacket with shiny gold buttons. Such a lovely thing—that jacket. I always did say one day I'd have me one so fine. Anyhow, Crackers dropped bits of crackers to form a trail, and the monkey found it and followed. The four of us had a grand time with that monkey before the organ grinder caught us and give it to us good."

"Four of you? You mentioned only three."

Darcy's expression sobered. "There was another. Roger had a crippled leg after falling off a wall. Sometimes Crackers and Hunstable took turns carrying him on their backs when Roger got tired of walkin' with his stick. Roger couldn't steal nothin' for the gang, bein' a cripple like he was, but we took care of him. He was four years younger than me, like me own little brother."

"And where is he now? Still in London, I presume?"

She stared into the fire. "Roger weren't strong. One hard winter, he died."

Brent flinched. Her soft, short sentences revealed more than she was aware. He had no experience when it came to offering sympathy—especially to young women—and felt completely out of his element.

"I see. Well, at least you seem to have a few good memories," he said lamely.

A smile lit her face again. "I do at that. So tell me, Guv'ner, have you any brothers or sisters?"

The question hit Brent like a slap in the face. He'd never talked to anyone about Bill, though Stewart, of course, knew the basic facts. Yet something had happened between him and Darcy in these last few minutes, something that had strangely and irrevocably drawn them closer together. She had shared a painful portion of her life, and Brent felt he should reciprocate.

Before he could question his rash decision, he spoke. "I have one brother. Bill left home when he was fifteen and later joined up with a felon who ran a numbers racket. I talked to

Bill once, almost a year ago. He sent me a letter and asked me to meet him in Manhattan."

Brent sighed, took off his spectacles, and wiped them with a handkerchief. "I tried to talk to him, to persuade him to listen to reason, but he would have none of it."

◈

Darcy had no idea what a numbers racket was, but it must be awful from the look on Brent's face. "I'm sorry, Guv'ner. I'll ask the good Lord to keep a watch on 'im."

He lifted his startled gaze. "Thank you, Miss Evans. I would appreciate your intercession."

Her tentative grin evolved into a full-blown smile. "Well, not sure I know what that fancy word means—my, but you know a lot of 'em! But if it means prayin', then you can count on me for that, Guv'ner."

He continued to look at her, his eyes almost tender. "Yes, I believe I can. From what I've seen, you are a most dependable young woman." He cleared his throat, as if embarrassed, and stood. "I should return to my quarters. A blessed Christmas to you, Miss Evans. Incidentally, your reading is much improved." He moved hurriedly to the foyer, grabbed his hat and coat, and walked out into the swirling bits of light snow.

"And a blessed Christmas to you, Guv'ner," Darcy murmured, feeling as if she'd just received an unexpected gift. She stared at the closed door, took the last bite of her apple, then headed to the kitchen to help Irma with the dishes—and maybe sneak another slice of that fruitcake Irma had made.

◈

January and February brought more snow. The old potbellied stove that warmed the schoolhouse malfunctioned, spewing out gray smoke and sending everyone outside into the frigid air, coughing and hacking.

To the best of Brent's analysis, something had gotten clogged high in the stovepipe—too high to remove. Since none of the men were adept at fixing things, they decided to wait until spring to either have the fifty-year-old stove repaired or buy a new one. In the meantime, Brent relocated to an empty room in the boys' wing of the main house. To have him so near day in and day out flustered Darcy, and she often found herself dropping things or saying things she shouldn't.

Lessons continued, though not with the previous school-room order, since teaching was administered in the parlor. The boys sat on the sofa, chairs, carpeting—wherever they could find a spot—and took their lessons from Brent. Reading and reciting filled long hours. When they weren't studying, they did their chores. Yet with nine boys and five adults sharing a minimal amount of space for weeks on end, petty fights soon erupted. Tonight, Darcy happened to be the only adult in the room.

She wrapped her short arms around Joel's slim waist and, with as much brute strength as she could muster, pulled the wiry lad off Herbert while the two other boys in the room stood and watched. The redhead had a black eye. Once Darcy released Joel, Herbert flew at the blond scamp.

"Oh, no, you don't!" Darcy clutched a handful of the boy's collar at the back. He fought to break loose, hurling malicious threats and trying to lash out at Joel, whose face bore nary a scratch.

"What's going on here? I heard the ruckus from all the way upstairs." Charleigh hurried into the room, her skirts clutched in both hands. Seeing the troublemakers, her mouth thinned. "Joel, you may march yourself into Mr. Lyons's office this minute. Herbert, tell Irma to fetch you a steak for that eye; then you may join Joel."

"He started it," Herbert whined.

"Hardly," Joel shot back.

"I don't care who started it! Do you hear? *I don't care.*" Charleigh's eyes shot sparks and her breathing was labored. "Furthermore, I don't wish to hear another word out of either of you or you'll get extra job duties for a month. Now, go."

Flabbergasted, Darcy stared at her friend. Charleigh was usually so calm when dealing with the boys. Yet tonight she looked as if she were ready to rake the whole lot of them over flaming coals.

Samuel, the young man who'd come to the Refuge after the war, hurried into the room, followed by three of the boys. Upon seeing the situation, he herded the children out, also putting a firm hand to both Joel's and Herbert's shoulders to prevent further fighting.

Darcy moved to stand in front of her friend. "Charleigh," she said, her voice low, "what's ailin' you?"

"How did you—I mean, why should you think something's ailing me?" Charleigh averted her gaze to the fireplace.

"I've known you too long, Luv. Now, let's go make us a nice cup of tea, and you can tell me all about it." Putting an arm around her friend's shoulders, Darcy steered Charleigh toward the kitchen. "I made some lovely apple cinnamon muffins this morning too."

They found the room unoccupied; and Darcy set about fixing the promised tea, though she noticed a coffeepot warming on the stove, probably left there by Irma. Darcy wrinkled her nose. She preferred tea with plenty of lemon.

Once the beverage was made, Darcy set a muffin in front of her friend, grabbed an orange from the bowl, and took a seat across from Charleigh. "Now, tell me what has you flutterin' about like a mad, wet hen." The allusion didn't bring the desired smile Darcy hoped for.

With jerky movements, Charleigh plucked up her spoon, stirred, then set it back down on the saucer. Her eyes were full of pain when she looked up. "I think Stewart's leaving me."

"Leaving you?" Darcy repeated in disbelief.

She nodded. "The letter from his family was the excuse he needed. Oh, I don't mean to sound heartless—I do care about his father's health, and I know he needs to go to them. But, Darcy, I don't think he's coming back. I failed him, you see, and now he wants out."

"Failed him?" Darcy repeated, feeling like an echo.

Charleigh looked down. "I can't give him children. We've

been married four years, and in that time I've lost five babies. I–I never talked about my past when we were together at Turreney Farm, I know."

Darcy waited, expectant. Charleigh had been close mouthed about her private life and why she'd been sentenced. Darcy never asked, since it had been an unspoken code among the convicts to mind one's own affairs. But she'd always wondered.

Charleigh released her breath in a heavy sigh. "In a nutshell, I lived with a man—a criminal—for three years. I thought we were married but came to find out the ceremony was a sham." She paused, obviously finding it difficult to say the rest. "The night the *Titanic* sank, he beat me; and the next morning, on the *Carpathia*, I miscarried our child."

Darcy listened, stunned.

Tear-filled eyes looked into her own. "Eric ruined me, Darcy. I've known it for some time. It's because of him and his abuse that I can't have children. And Stewart wants a son and daughter so badly. What am I to do? I'm losing my husband, and I'm helpless to do anything about it." She buried her face in her hands, sobbing quietly.

Darcy vacated her chair and knelt beside her friend, putting her arm around Charleigh's shoulders. "You're wrong, Luv. Stewart adores you. Why, just to look in the man's eyes I can see as plain as the nose on me face that he's smitten with you."

Charleigh didn't answer.

"He feels duty-bound to help his family but is obviously torn on the proper thing to do. Go to them or stay home with you, his wife."

"I suppose. But, Darcy, what if he decides to go and doesn't come back? We've. . ." She looked down at her lap. "We've quarreled lately. Since he came home from the war, he doesn't act the same. He rarely talks to me anymore, and I feel it's because he wishes he'd never married me."

"I disagree." Darcy laid her other hand over her friend's cold one. "War changes people, Luv. There's no tellin' what Stewart saw in France. Give it time. And, Charleigh, you need to seek the faith that ye somehow lost and start believin' God to work things out. I'm not too smart yet on how one's supposed to act as a Christian, but I do pray for everyone in this house each and every night."

A wisp of a smile tugged at Charleigh's lips. "Oh, Darcy, you're such a dear friend." Her eyelashes flitted down, then up, her expression guilty. "Unfortunately, I can't say the same about me. I was overbearing when you first came. I'm afraid I've grown accustomed to supervising nine boys with criminal records and have become domineering in my attitude. Forgive me for not asking if you wanted to change rather than practically ordering you to do so."

"Oh, but I'm not angered, Charleigh," Darcy was quick to assure. "Not one bit. So don't you worry none. Actually, I'm glad you forced me hand. I never would've had the courage to ask the favor for meself—since I felt beholden to you for bringin' me here all the way from London. And you were right; it never hurts to gain head knowledge."

Charleigh smiled. "For being four years younger than I, you're so much wiser, Darcy."

"Maybe in some things but not in others. Even with the trainin' you've given me, I still have problems with the way I talk; and I often find meself sayin' things that make Mr. Thomas's hair about turn white, judgin' from the shock that suddenly sweeps 'cross his face. Have you ever seen his mouth drop open? Sure is a sight for such a dignified gent!"

Charleigh giggled, the sound cheering Darcy. Her friend would be all right. She was a survivor, as was Darcy.

"I'll admit, and please don't take this wrong, but seeing the two of you together is—how do I put this? Amusing at times." Charleigh's eyes sparkled with more than tears. "Frankly, I'm amazed at how well you've both gotten along lately—for being such total opposites, I mean."

Darcy returned to her seat. She stirred the cooling liquid, wishing the sudden fire in her cheeks would cool as well. "He's a fine sort of fellow." She took a sip from her cup and began to peel her orange. "A good teacher."

"Yes, he is that," Charleigh agreed, her expression softly probing, as though she could sense more than Darcy was willing to reveal.

Darcy took her full cup to the basin. "Well, I'm a mite tired, and I have lessons to complete besides. You'd think Brent would ease up, what with the cabin fever everyone's had lately. . . ." Her words trailed off when she realized her slip. She'd never before used his Christian name in conversation. She only hoped Charleigh hadn't noticed. Hesitant, she turned.

Charleigh's smile was wide. "Yes, Brent can be rather dogmatic when it comes to schooling. He's just what those boys need. And what you need."

Darcy's ears grew hot. "He's helped quite a bit in teaching me to read and write; that's a fact."

Charleigh rose and looped an arm around Darcy's shoulders. "I know you like him, Darcy, and I think that's 'nifty,' as Tommy would say. So do stop trying to cover up. I'm one hundred percent in favor of you and Brent forming a more serious relationship, if that's what has you so flustered."

As she finished her last sentence, Brent strode into the kitchen. Darcy almost died from humiliation when she realized from the startled expression on his reddening face that he'd heard every word.

# five

Brent stopped, stared, and wondered what to do. Despite the chill in the house, his neck and face burned. He deliberated on the most appropriate way to extricate himself from this latest embarrassing predicament. That they knew he'd overheard Charleigh's shocking statement was obvious, judging from the way Darcy's face flamed poppy red.

"Excuse me," Darcy mumbled, hurrying past Brent. "I need to be about me business."

Relief mingled with an underlying sense of empathy. After all, the shocking words hadn't been Darcy's. He imagined she was as unnerved by them as he. Why Charleigh had even said such a thing was beyond Brent's reasoning. He swiveled to look at her.

Charleigh's gaze turned from the spot where Darcy had exited and met his own. She seemed ill at ease, repentant. "I should check on the boys." Before she moved through the doorway, she offered Brent an uncertain smile. "Good night."

Alone at last, Brent shook his head, let out a prolonged breath, and set his briefcase on the table. His disloyal mind replayed Charleigh's words, and he gave a short laugh. The idea of him and Darcy as a couple was so—so preposterous, so outlandish, so altogether incongruous that Brent didn't dwell on the picture overly long.

Instead, he moved to pour himself a cup of the strong coffee that good-hearted Irma had left on the stove. He needed something to help him keep alert while grading papers, and Brent didn't share Darcy's preference for tea.

Sitting at the table, he noticed her half-peeled orange and stared at it a few seconds—imagining her popping one of the segments into her mouth and then grinning at him. Abruptly he turned his attention to the first paper with a scowl. He must wrest his mind off Darcy Evans and apply it to the task at hand.

The short, quirky sentences and frequent blobs of ink testified to Joel's handiwork without Brent needing to look in the upper right-hand corner for the name. The boy was always trying to get away with the least amount of effort possible. The original poem was half the five stanzas of the story poem Brent had assigned, didn't rhyme, and glorified a runaway involved in a life of crime.

Sighing, Brent made corrections, took off a large percentage for not following directions, and gave Joel a 49. He picked up the next paper in the stack, a slight smile on his lips.

At least Tommy did try, as evidenced by his laborious efforts at doing a job well. Several half-written words over the page were crossed out and reattempted, some as many as four times until the word was spelled and written correctly. The paper was messy with its many alterations, but the lad had persistence; Brent would grant him that. The poem was unusual, about a toad eating a lame mouse, but Brent didn't like to tamper with his students' creative abilities. He was more concerned with grammar and sentence structure at this stage of their education. Giving Tommy a 70, he went on to the next paper. He picked it up and froze.

Darcy's large block letters stared up at him. She hadn't learned cursive writing, though Brent had attempted to teach her. But she often balked and demanded to know why a person had to learn to write in two different styles "when one way of writin' was all a body needed."

Familiar sounds in the room—the sporadic drip from the water pump hitting the basin, the creaking of the timbered house settling, the barely audible moan of wind outside—faded into the background as his gaze traveled over the neatly printed poem:

*Let me tell you a story, a sad one, me friend,*
*About three young lads I knew in the East End,*
*Crackers was brite, often looking for a lark,*
*Hunstable was kwiet, but he had a certun spark,*
*Roger was gentel, a little lamb, and like no other,*
*And we all took good care of him as if he was our brother.*

*Most would call them feluns, for theevin' is what they done,*
*But the three of them became my friends when I had not a one.*
*For all his bluff and brashnuss, Crackers was a good leader of*
*   our gang,*
*'Til the day he was cot filchin' bread and was slammed in jail*
*   with a clang.*

*Hunstable changed once Crackers left, thoe he tried to take*
*   his place.*
*Once we were four, then we were three, 'til Hunstable vanisht*
*   with nary a trace.*
*And lastly there was dear Roger, a sweet angel in disgize,*
*Lame and sick, his stay weren't long, 'til one day he forever*
*   closed his eyes.*

*Yet the moral of me story, friend, has little to do with theevin',*
*Even those who don't know what the Good Book says know*
*   it's wrong to make a life out of steelin'.*
*Rather the messadge of me poem is this: Why did no one help*
*   us or care?*
*We was only children trying to servive in a world that was*
*   harsh and bare.*

*Didn't peepul who read the Good Book see that it said to help*
*   the orfuns and needy?*
*Or did they just think us worthluss guttersnipes who was*
*   nothin' but dirty and greedy?*
*I don't know the answer, friend, thoe I've long tried to find*
*   the reezin;*

*But this I know, while I draw breath on this earth, I'll do*
*what I can for those who be needin'.*
*For each time I look on a poor child's face or that of a sad little*
*orfun,*
*I see me old friends, and remember our life, on the streets in the*
*East End of London.*

Brent blinked away the unexpected moisture that had sprung to his eyes. Never mind the misspelled words—they were of little significance in relation to the gold mine he'd struck. Darcy had talent. Her prose was a bit rough, but the artistic content was very good for a beginner's first poem. It further shocked him to realize they shared a knack for writing poetry, though Brent could see from this first attempt that Darcy's skill might well exceed his someday. Mechanics could be taught. Talent could not.

He pondered the printed words, wondering what had happened to her friends. Reading over the poem again, he fiddled with the paper, considering. An idea came to mind that made him smile. He measured the possibility awhile longer, then swept the rest of the papers into his briefcase, placing Darcy's ungraded one on top. Closing his portfolio, he grabbed it and hurried to the parlor, hoping he could find the form he'd come across in last week's *Saturday Evening Post*.

❧

Darcy stood at the open attic window, inhaling the fresh, bracing air that heralded the coming of spring. Clumps of bright green broke through the melting snow, which lay in patches over the dark earth. She watched Joel and Chris, a quiet, skinny boy with an unruly shock of blond hair, as they made their way toward the barn with buckets, probably to milk the two cows.

Darcy wrinkled her brow in concern. Lately, Joel seemed edgy, a container of pent-up energy waiting for a place to unleash. Of course, they all were anxious to spend time outside, having been holed up for most of the winter; but Joel seemed more volatile than the other boys.

Darcy smiled. Volatile. Her new word for the day. Every day she learned a different fancy word—one that Brent might use—in her efforts to increase her head knowledge. Maybe if she became more fancified, Brent might like her better.

The stray thought made her face go hot. Although behind his back the boys labeled Brent "a stick in the mud"—and rightly so—Darcy harbored a strong liking for the man ever since they'd talked last Christmas. She didn't care all that much if he was a bit stuffy and overly neat; yet Darcy knew he would never put up with the likes of her.

Sighing, she wished she could be more like Charleigh, who talked so properlike and was genteel, a real lady. Darcy often found herself doing things and later finding out it wasn't considered appropriate. Nor had her rough, Cockney accent disappeared, though at least her words were more easily understood.

Determined to have a quick romp with the boys in the cheery spring day, Darcy headed for the door and down the stairs. She should help Irma with the bread pudding, but the weather was too fine to waste.

Before Darcy could reach the threshold, Charleigh came around the corner. Her eyes were dark in her strained, white face.

"Charleigh, Luv, what's wrong?" Darcy gripped her friend's shoulders. She gave Charleigh a slight shake when she only stared. "Tell me! Ye look like ye've just seen a man leave his grave."

"A telegram came," Charleigh said, tears filling her eyes. "Stewart's father is deathly ill. . .something to do with his heart. Stewart is packing and leaving on the first train tomorrow."

"Oh, I am sorry!" Darcy pulled her friend into a hug.

"Oh, Darcy," Charleigh mumbled against the wide collar of Darcy's dress. "I'm trying to be brave, like a good wife should act. . .but. . .I just don't feel well."

Before Darcy could question her, Charleigh clutched Darcy's shoulder and collapsed in a faint against her.

❧

Brent stood outside with Stewart and watched the boys do their chores. Stewart frowned on hiring guards, insisting that the unusual way he and Charleigh ran the institution was how they felt the Lord had instructed them to do it. Brent had to admit the experimental method worked well. Though some of the older families in Sothsby, whose generations dated back to the 1700s, still opposed having a reformatory there, the community as a whole hadn't outwardly rebelled.

Except for minor infractions, there had never been a need for corporal punishment. Once a new boy tried to run away, but he hadn't gotten far before Stewart found him. Now Lance seemed content at the reform. He never tried to escape again, and his tendency to withdraw from others had dissipated.

Brent watched Lance as he helped Samuel fix a broken porch rail. The weak sun shone over Lance's freckled face and strong body—worlds removed from the grubby, pale scarecrow who'd come to their doorstep years ago.

"I don't like leaving Charleigh," Stewart said, breaking into Brent's reverie. "But I have to do what I feel is right, just as she had to do years ago when she turned herself over to Scotland Yard."

"I agree."

Obviously still troubled, Stewart rotated the brim of his straw boater. "My family needs my legal counsel. Mother is helpless when it comes to dealing with business matters of any sort; and with Father bedridden, she's frightened they'll lose the store." He sounded as if he were trying hard to convince himself that he was doing the right thing. "Still, I'm worried about Charleigh. She had a fainting spell yesterday—which is so unlike her—though she didn't tell me a word about it. I had to hear the news from Darcy." Frowning, he looked off into the distance. "Charleigh's been under a great deal of strain, and I fear she's taken on too much with the boys and the upkeep of the house. She needs rest."

"I'll look after her welfare, as I'm sure Miss Evans will.

Those two are close."

Stewart offered him a weak smile. "You don't know what a relief it is to hear you say that. And I'm doubly glad we sent for Charleigh's friend."

The front door opened and both women appeared. Brent noticed Charleigh slip her hand from Darcy's and straighten her shoulders. "The train will be leaving in a little over an hour," she said in a small brave voice. Her smile wavered. Darcy stepped up and said something close to her ear. Charleigh gave a brief nod and tacked a tight smile to her face. "Shall we go?"

❧

The ride to Ithaca was fraught with tension. False smiles were tossed about, and forced laughter crackled the air, feeling almost tangible and grating against raw nerves. Words of little import filled rare interludes of quiet.

As they neared town, Darcy noticed several people standing on the platform, waiting to say good-bye to loved ones and friends or to welcome those arriving. A small group of rowdy young men burst into raucous song that sounded better suited to a tavern.

Darcy stared at the trio, receiving a wink from a cheeky blond gent in return. Much to her shock, Brent grabbed her above the elbow once she alighted from the wagon and hurried her along after Stewart and Charleigh. What was even more of a surprise, he didn't release her once they came to the platform and stopped a short distance from the two, to give their friends a measure of privacy.

Darcy wasn't sure what to think. She wondered if it was wrong to enjoy him standing so close, his warm fingers wrapped around her sleeve, when Charleigh was depressed, uncertain if she'd ever see her husband again.

Darcy sobered. Charleigh had been quiet all afternoon, and Darcy knew that she and Stewart had argued last night. She'd heard them from her attic room.

Watching them now, Stewart seemed stiff, almost cold, and Charleigh appeared resigned. Darcy prayed that Stewart wouldn't leave Charleigh, as Darcy's own papa had left her mother when Darcy was all of five years. The war had obviously changed Stewart. Darcy was glad that Brent had been exempted, as Charleigh once informed her; and without meaning to, she voiced the thought aloud.

"What did you say?" Brent asked.

Darcy looked at him. "I was just sorry for them two and wishing they could make it right between them again," she blurted. "And I said I'm thankful, I am, that you weren't sent off to fight in the war—and aren't dealing with your own sufferings now because of it."

His eyes widened behind the spectacles. Darcy inwardly cringed. Would she ever learn to think before she spoke?

Brent's face went a shade darker. "Yes, well, thank you for the sentiment, Miss Evans." He cleared his throat, looking everywhere but at her.

Darcy's gaze slid down his long nose to his well-shaped lips. Idly, she wondered what it would feel like to kiss this man. Crackers sometimes kissed her on the forehead when she was sad, but that wasn't the same. They'd only been children.

Nearby, a couple locked in a farewell embrace. For a fleeting moment, Darcy considered throwing her arms around Brent and giving him a quick peck on the lips. Wouldn't that make his mouth drop open! The thought made her giggle.

Brent looked at her. "Something amuses you, Miss Evans?"

"Nothin', Guv'ner. Nothin' ter squawk habout anyways," she deliberately replied in heavy Cockney, her smile wide.

His gaze softened, and Darcy was sure he was remembering their first meeting a little less than a year ago at this train station.

"I never told you," he said, his voice quiet, "how impressed I am with how far you've come in such a short time. You're a remarkable student."

Darcy managed not to let the smile slip from her face. Did he only approve of her now that she'd learned to talk right—well, almost right? The thought was disappointing. She wanted him to like her for the person she was on the inside. Not just for what she was being transformed into on the outside.

The train's warning whistle pierced the air, startling both Darcy and Brent. He stepped a few feet away, his actions almost self-conscious, and looked elsewhere. Darcy glanced toward Charleigh and Stewart and was relieved to see him draw his wife into his arms.

A tall, dark-haired young man in a drab uniform drew Darcy's attention as he stepped off the train. He returned her stare, then strode her way, a sly grin on his thin features. "Well, he-l-loo, sweet tomato. How's about a welcome-home hug for a returning doughboy?"

Darcy blinked. "Are ye talkin' to me?"

"I sure am, Sugar—British sugar, unless I miss my guess." He rested his free hand on the post behind her, casually leaning her way. "So where do you hail from, sweet thing? I don't seem to remember seeing you in our small town."

"Sir, I shall have to ask you to leave the lady alone."

Brent's stern voice sounded from behind Darcy's right shoulder.

The man gave Brent a quick upward flick of his eyes. "This is between the lady and me," he said. He leaned closer to Darcy, eyeing her as if she were a choice cut of beefsteak. She smelled sour whiskey on his breath. "How's about you and me leaving this crummy dump and getting to know one another better?"

"Sir!" Brent protested.

"Aw, why don't you dry up," the stranger growled in disgust.

Before she could push him away, Darcy watched as the top half of a black umbrella whammed the man's shoulder from behind. He jumped and turned, fists raised. A short woman with white ringlets jiggling around her wrinkled face wagged a finger in his face, and he dropped his arms to his side in apparent shock.

"Clarence Lockhurst, you leave that poor young lady alone and apologize this instant," she said in a voice still strong for her advanced years. "You've been nothing but trouble since I had you as a student in my fourth-grade class. I had hoped that serving in the war might improve your disposition, if nothing else." Her strict countenance melted into a grudging smile. "Still, it's nice to see that the Germans didn't shoot you full of holes. Though you'll likely give your mother a case of the vapors, arriving like this without warning. But at least you made it home from that horrid hospital. Now come along. It's a good thing I came to see my niece off, or I might not have run into you."

"Yes, Miss Finnelton," the man muttered, and the woman walked away, obviously expecting him to follow. He seemed embarrassed, his gaze flitting to the platform before returning to Darcy again. He shrugged. "Sorry, Miss. I was only trying to have a little fun. No harm intended."

"Clarence!" the woman called without slowing her pace.

Darcy watched in disbelief as the tall young man hurried after the diminutive old woman like a truant child. Somewhat amused by the spectacle, she turned to Brent. The words on her lips died when she saw anger flash in his eyes. Confused, she wondered if his ire was directed at her. Did he think she'd encouraged that man's advances? Did he care?

"Stewart is ready to board," he said through tight lips. "Charleigh needs us."

Darcy blinked in surprise. This was the first time she'd heard Brent use their Christian names. Likely because his emotions were running high, he hadn't been aware of the slip. Darcy just wished it could have been her name that rolled so easily off his tongue.

❧

The months seemed to fly by. Summer chased spring away, and the cool winds of autumn blew in early. Darcy had been at the Refuge almost an entire year, and in that time she had learned much—especially the meaning of true Christianity. It was more than the prayer she'd spoken at Turreney Farm, accepting Jesus as her Savior. It was a walk she needed to take every day of her life.

She looked with concern to the closed schoolhouse door. Brent was late. For the prompt schoolmaster to be tardy was tantamount to a major crisis. She wrinkled her brow as her thoughts drifted to Charleigh. These past months in Stewart's absence her friend had become a pale ghost, quiet, so much different from the Charleigh that Darcy had met years ago and come to love. Her faith in God was suffering too, and Darcy didn't know how to help her, except to pray and be there for her when she could.

The boys' chatter and guffaws dwindled as the door opened, letting in pale September light—and Brent.

He carried a folded magazine and smiled, looking her way. Darcy's heart lurched in uncertainty mixed with an odd feeling of expectation.

Taking his place at the front of the room, Brent eyed the class. "I have an announcement, but first I want you to hear something."

He opened the magazine, whose cover bore a color illustration by Norman Rockwell. Then, to Darcy's astonishment, he read the poem she'd written months ago. Only the words sounded more proper, or maybe it was hearing them in Brent's polished Eastern accent that made the difference.

When he finished, he smiled at her. "Miss Evans, I suppose I should first ask your apology for submitting your poem without permission to a local contest the *Saturday Evening Post* was sponsoring this past spring. In defense of my decision, I didn't want to unnecessarily raise your hopes, and as your tutor I acted—perhaps rashly, but it is done. I also took the liberty of correcting misspelled words, as well as a few small grammatical errors, before sending in your poem. I hope you'll forgive me. Based on prior contests, I knew they would judge heavily on content, and on those grounds I decided to enter your poem."

Darcy blinked, trying to comprehend all he said. He was asking that she forgive him for correcting her assignment? And for sending it to a local magazine?

She watched Brent walk to the desk that had been specially made for her, while pulling an envelope from his pocket. His blue eyes sparkled as he set the envelope on her desktop.

"It's my pleasure to inform you that you've won second place in the beginner's category of the contest, the prize being eight dollars."

Gasps filtered through the room. Eight dollars? Whatever would she do with such wealth? She'd never had anything in her life, and now to be given this. . .

With saucerlike eyes, she stared at the envelope.

"What're ya gonna do with all that money, Darcy?" Tommy asked softly in wonder.

"I'll bet she's gonna buy them glad rags with all the bows and fripperies she was eyeing in that lady magazine the other day," another voice piped up. "So she can be all purty-fied for certain people."

Darcy ignored Joel's mocking words and the giggles that greeted his reply. Instead she looked up at Brent, still feeling as if she were in a dream. "May I tell Charleigh?" she asked, her question coming out in a squeak. She cleared her throat and lowered her voice a notch. "It might cheer her to know her idea of me learning brought about some good."

Brent turned his stern countenance from Joel to her, and his expression softened. "Of course, Miss Evans. You may be excused."

Sliding from her seat, Darcy grasped the envelope as though it might evaporate into thin air. The smoothness of the fine-grained paper assured her it was indeed real, and her fingers clutched it more tightly. At the door she stopped and looked at Brent. His gaze still rested on her.

"Thank you, Guv'ner, for sendin' in me poem. But most of all thank you for believin' in me," she managed before hurrying out the door.

Her mind played havoc with her heart. Why had he done it? Was there more to this gesture than a schoolmaster supporting a student? Could he, by chance, be starting to care for her?

Knowing she'd find Charleigh in her room this time of day, where she often sequestered herself now that Stewart was gone, Darcy sped up the stairs by twos. Whatever would she do with all this money? She hoped her good fortune would bring a smile to Charleigh's face. Should she also tell Charleigh how she felt about Brent, though her friend had already guessed? They'd never discussed him since the night he'd caught Charleigh and Darcy talking in the kitchen. All this time, Darcy felt she hadn't any chance with Brent. But after doing such a nice thing for her and after the way he'd looked at her when he gave her the envelope—maybe he did care.

Outside Charleigh's room, Darcy knocked. She didn't wait for an answer but opened the door and stepped inside, her mind so filled with conflicting thoughts that she didn't stop to consider that she was barging in without invitation.

Charleigh halted in the process of retrieving her dressing gown from the back of the chair. Her long nightgown detailed her rounded stomach.

Darcy inhaled swiftly, her gaze lifting to Charleigh's. "Why-ever didn't you tell me?"

Charleigh released a weary breath and sank to the edge of the bed.

Her own news forgotten, Darcy closed the door, pocketed the envelope, and hurried to sit beside her friend. She looped an arm around her shoulders. "Does Stewart know?"

"I couldn't tell him. Not after losing the others. And with his father's recent death, he has so much on his mind as it is." Charleigh hesitated. "And I couldn't tell him before he left because I didn't want to use the baby as a means of keeping him here."

"You've known that long?"

"I suspected it."

"Oh, Charleigh, that's why you fainted that day, isn't it?" Darcy should have realized, though with Charleigh's plump form and roomy-waisted dresses it had been difficult to tell. "Have you been to see a doctor?"

"No. I suppose I should."

"Yes, you should," Darcy stated firmly. "And what's more, you should stay off your feet. I'll take over your duties until the babe comes." The prospect was daunting, but Darcy had observed Charleigh often in the year she'd been at Lyons's Refuge. With Irma and Brent's help, surely they could keep things running smoothly so Charleigh could get the rest she needed.

"I'm frightened." Charleigh turned wide green eyes her way. "I don't think I could stand to lose another child. To have a doctor tell me there's no hope for this one either. I—I've never been this far along—" Her voice broke.

Darcy grasped Charleigh's cold hand and squeezed it. "There, there, Luv. That's no way to think. Between us, we'll pray that the good Lord protects the wee babe and brings it safely into the world in due time." She hesitated. "Do you know when that might be, by chance?"

Charleigh looked away. "In December, I think. Near Christmas."

"I'll have Irma call and see if the doctor can come today. You stay in bed and rest. You're looking a mite pale. I'll take care of everything."

"Oh, Darcy. I don't know what I'd do without you. You're so strong, and lately I feel as if my strength is seeping away. I've found it harder and harder to trust God." The admission was made with shame.

Darcy gave her friend an encouraging smile. "Well, then, we'll see what we can do to boost your faith again, shall we?" Like a mother hen, Darcy ushered Charleigh under the sheets and tucked her in. "But for now get some rest. And don't you worry about a thing, Luv. Darcy has everything under control."

She almost believed her bold statement. Keeping the assured look on her face until she closed the door behind her, Darcy prayed, "Oh, Lord, I'm sure going to be needin' Your help. And help me friend, Charleigh; give her peace. Help her babe to grow strong—"

The front door banged open. "Where is everybody?" Herbert's voice sailed up the stairwell. Knowing Herbert, who got into more trouble than Darcy could have believed possible, she was sure some minor injury needed tending to.

Darcy closed her eyes. "About that peace, Lord," she muttered, "I sure could be usin' a dose of it as well."

## six

The early October sun did what little it could to warm his back as Brent left the schoolroom. He had no idea what to do about Joel—about half the class, really. With Stewart's absence and Charleigh bedridden due to strict orders from the doctor, the boys took advantage of Brent. It seemed a day didn't pass that one of them wasn't disciplined for infractions inside and outside the classroom.

Brent rounded the schoolhouse, wondering how to handle the issue. Michael had moved to Lyons's Refuge with his wife to offer aid as well as reinforcement. Though Charleigh's father was tenderhearted to the lads, his massive size and gruff voice let them know he wasn't someone to cross. Yet Brent didn't want to run to Michael every time one of the boys misbehaved. Surely Brent was man enough to take on nine lads smaller than he?

Remembering the altercation at the train station with the man who'd accosted Darcy, Brent pressed his lips together. He hadn't been able to help her. The one brief look the loutish man had tossed his way made it clear he thought Brent lacking in the area of fisticuffs. Not that Brent had desired a fight—quite the opposite. But it stung that a stranger thought him unable to protect and that an elderly woman wielding an umbrella had exhibited more courage than Brent.

He halted suddenly, spotting Darcy and four boys across the expanse of yard, underneath the shedding oaks. The rakes they'd been using lay propped against the massive trunks, forgotten. All five were cavorting, chasing one another and dumping handfuls of brown, crimson, and yellow leaves on unsuspecting heads.

Brent sighed and crossed his arms over his chest. Why

should it surprise him to see Darcy in such a role, rather than the one she should be adopting—that of overseeing the boys' chores? As Brent watched, Lance came at her from behind with a pail and showered her head with leaves at the same time Tommy bent to the ground and sprayed her with leaves from the front.

"Aaaeee," she squealed, her Cockney coming to the fore. "I'll see ever' one o' you scrubbin' floors, I will! And that'll be after ye rake the yard. So ye think ye can get the best o' Darcy Evans, do you?" Swiftly she changed direction, going after Lance. He shrieked and ran but didn't get far before she tackled him as if she were a football player and not a woman wearing a dress. They both went laughing and rolling into the only pile of raked leaves—scattering them. Red, yellow, and brown vegetation flew everywhere.

Shaking his head, Brent closed his eyes.

"Hey, Guv'ner!" Darcy's cry sliced through the cool air. Brent grimaced at the annoying name she persisted in calling him but looked her way.

"Come join us!" She scooped up an armful of rich autumn colors and sent her bounty sailing into the air, with the abandonment of a gleeful child. "The leaves are fine. Crisp and crackly—perfect for rollin' about. So what say? Care to join in the tussle?"

"Join in the. . . ," he repeated quietly in shocked disbelief. With a shake of his head, he moved in the direction of the schoolroom. The four walls offered safety, sanity. He had enough troubles; no need to invite more.

Rapid crunching sounded behind him, growing louder. "Hey, Guv'ner—don't leave yet!" Darcy's voice was breathless.

Knowing that the sensible thing would be to keep walking—before he was attacked from behind with a bucketful of leaves—Brent increased his pace, almost to a jog. She grabbed his sleeve and pulled. He whirled and hastily brought up a hand to block his eyes, expecting a smattering of leaves to dash him in the face. The action unbalanced them, and Darcy tumbled against his chest, almost sending them both to the ground.

In a reflexive act, Brent threw his arms around her at the same time she grabbed handfuls of his vest. An electrified moment elapsed before she lifted her stunned gaze. Equally shocked, he stared down at velvety eyes rimmed with black curly lashes. Eyes so dark, they held traces of deep, mesmerizing blue-purple.

"Hey! Look at Teacher and Miz Darcy," Ralph's voice piped up. "Reckon Joel was right and they'll be smoochin' in the cloakroom next?"

A chorus of chortles met his question.

Heat racing to his face, Brent dropped his arms from around Darcy's waist and stepped as far back as he could. She still clutched his vest, his shirt underneath, and one suspender.

"Miss Evans!" he exclaimed. "Would you mind releasing your hold?"

"What?" She blinked as if coming out of a stupor. "Oh, sorry!" She let go.

The suspender snapped back into place with a sting. By this time, the giggles from the boys had turned into rip-roaring laughter.

"Excuse me. I've business to attend." Brent turned and again headed for the safety of the schoolhouse.

"But, Guv'ner. . ."

With his back to her, he hastily tucked in the few inches of shirt material that bagged loose above his high-waisted trousers. Once through the door, he sensed her presence behind him. He was sure of it when she barreled into him, stepping on his heels as he came to a stop.

Nowhere was safe any longer.

Letting out a slow breath for patience, he faced her. "Yes? You wish to speak with me?"

A sheepish expression crossed her pink face, now shiny from her exertions. With bits of colored leaves in her disheveled hair and clinging to her skirt, she looked little more than a girl. "I'm sorry, Guv'ner. Really I ham. But you walk so fast!"

"Apology accepted," he said quickly. When she didn't move to go, he lifted his brow. "Was there something else?"

She crossed her arms and cocked her head to the side, all awkwardness leaving her as she observed him. "Tell me, Guv'ner, why is it you don't like to have fun?"

"Excuse me?"

She rolled her eyes and shook her head. "Do I have to spell it out for you like I did last Christmas? Ever since I've known you, you do nothin' more than work, eat, and sleep. I've never seen you unbend—not once mind you—and have a good time."

Brent cleared his throat. "Perhaps your definition of fun doesn't coincide with mine."

"Okay, what's your definition?"

Brent opened his mouth to reply, then stopped to consider.

"Aha! See there? You don't even know what fun is!"

"I most certainly do." He removed his spectacles, grabbed his handkerchief from his pocket, and angrily swiped at the spotless lenses. "I just don't feel the need to reply to your query."

"And I'll bet my eyeteeth it's 'cause you don't know the answer."

"Miss Evans."

"Mr. Thomas."

Brent blinked, more stunned that she'd finally called him by his proper name than by her mimicking behavior.

She uncrossed her arms, a sly smile lifting her lips. "All right then. Prove it."

"Excuse me?"

"Prove to me that you can have fun."

Brent gave a curt shake of his head. "I hardly think a child-ish display of frolicking about in dead vegetation befits a schoolmaster of nine young boys."

She waved a dismissive hand. "I'm not talking about that. I have somethin' else in mind."

Unease crept up Brent's spine at the sudden speculating

gleam in her eye. "Such as?"

"Two things really. Take part in the fence-paintin' contest we're havin' on Friday."

Brent considered. He could referee without actually having to be involved in what promised to be a messy undertaking. "Agreed. And the second?"

"I need your help with an idea for keepin' the boys in line. It's what I wanted to talk to you about in the first place." She swept past him toward the front of the schoolroom.

Puzzled, Brent turned and watched as she propped herself on the edge of his desk.

"Better take a seat, Guv'ner. I have a feelin' this will do more than just make your mouth pop open."

&

Brent stared at her with uncertainty and approached slowly, his eyes wary. He still hadn't replaced his spectacles, and Darcy again thought what nice blue eyes he had. Instead of taking his usual place behind his desk, he walked to her small writing table six feet away, pulled out the chair, and sat down.

Darcy swiveled on his desk to face him.

"Well?" Brent asked.

"Just thinkin' how to put it best," she murmured. "All right, it's like this. When I was in town with Michael and Alice, gettin' supplies and such, I heard news of a carnival comin' to a neighborin' town next month. Now, bein' as I had no idea what a carnival was, mind you, I did some askin', and the storekeeper told me."

"A carnival?" Brent asked, already suspecting the worst.

Darcy shrugged one shoulder. "It's all on the up-and-up. I thought we could use the carnival as an incentive for the boys. A goal to help them show good behavior and keep up with their studies—that sort of thing."

Brent stared at her incredulously. "And just who do you propose to take nine miniature hooligans, still in the process of being reformed, out of the boundaries of Lyons's Refuge and to a frivolous function held in an unsuspecting town?"

"Why, you, of course. And me. And maybe Michael." She smiled as his eyes widened. "But it would just be three boys, not nine. The three who try the hardest and show the most progress. Like winnin' a contest, such as I did with that poetry one. That's where I got the idea."

Brent only stared. After several seconds elapsed, he shook his head. "That's the most preposterous idea I've heard! As I'm certain you know by now, there are those who are dead-set against having a reformatory in this town—though the community as a whole hasn't rebelled. That we take the boys outside Lyons's Refuge for church on Sundays is difficult for many to tolerate. But to take them to a carnival?"

Her mouth thinning, Darcy stood and faced him squarely, planting her hands on her hips. "They's just little boys, Guv'ner. Little boys who had a hard lot in life and are payin' for their crimes. Why shouldn't they be allowed to 'ave a good time now and hagain, like other boys their age, 'specially if they be earnin' it?" Darcy forced herself to speak more slowly. When she was excited, she almost always slipped into her Cockney. "They'll be well supervised, one-on-one. So there'll be no shenanigans of any kind to worry about."

"But a *carnival?*" he stressed. "Now, I'll admit the fence-painting idea you devised is rather a good plan. It reminds me of a scene in a book by Mark Twain. However, a carnival is entirely out of the question. Not only would we most likely have to get permission from the judge who released the boys to our care, but there are other problems I foresee as well."

"Sure it isn't only 'cause you don't like ta have fun?" Darcy challenged.

He blew out a short breath. "Really, Miss Evans—"

"If I told you Charleigh was in favor of the idea, would that make you think twice?"

He halted whatever he was about to say. "You've talked to Mrs. Lyons about this?" At Darcy's abrupt nod, he lifted his brows in surprise. "And she agreed?"

"Most definitely. She said it was a smashing idea."

"And I thought she had more sense than that," Brent muttered, shaking his head and looking away. His gaze met hers again. "And Mr. Larkin? What does he say?"

"Michael was there when I talked to Charleigh. He thought the idea a grand one."

"He would." Brent slowly replaced his glasses. "It would appear that I'm outvoted by members of the board."

"Meaning?"

He looked at her, pained acceptance filling his eyes. "Meaning, Miss Evans, that in all likelihood we shall be attending a carnival."

❧

Late morning sunshine washed the grounds and the row of eager boys standing along the discolored wooden fence. Each lad held a paintbrush. Nine glowing, expectant faces turned toward Darcy, waiting for the signal. She eyed the row one more time to make certain everyone was in position, then cupped her hands around her mouth.

"Go!" she yelled.

Brushes plopped into pails of whitewash, and loud swishes of hard bristles on wood met her command. Gangly arms rapidly worked up and down as each boy painted his section of fence, striving to be the first to complete the contest. The winner would be awarded one of Darcy's famous blackberry pies all to himself. In addition, the winner would be given a free hour on Saturday while the other boys did their chores. Everyone who participated would receive a small prize—ribbons Darcy herself had made using Irma's box of sewing trinkets and scraps. Depending on how this first contest went, other contests might follow until all fences at Lyons's Refuge were whitewashed, a late task considering that freezing weather would soon be coming.

Darcy thought of something Charleigh said when Brent questioned her about the wisdom of issuing rewards for the contest. "All through the Bible the Lord blessed His children when they did what was right and good," Charleigh said. "And

He still does today. Children need a goal to work toward. Everyone does."

As Darcy watched the boys work, she pondered Charleigh's words. Darcy supposed her goal was to work at bettering herself and talking right. Charleigh's goal was to have a healthy baby. Stewart's goal was obviously to help his family, since his father's death. And Brent?

Darcy cast her gaze to where he stood between two myrtle trees. With his hands behind his back, he watched the contest a safe distance from the boys. What goals did Brent have? Likely, if he did entertain goals, they revolved around teaching his students and keeping the peace at Lyons's Refuge in Stewart's absence. Certainly his goals could have nothing to do with fun. The boys had long ago dubbed him "Ole-Stick-in-the-Mud-Thomas." Darcy pondered the term. Although Brent wasn't old, being in his mid-twenties if he were a day, seeing him standing there in his brown suit on the sodden ground, he did fit the adage well.

Darcy chuckled. The pleasant breeze must have carried the sound to Brent, for he turned his head to look. Seeing her gaze focused on him, he raised his brows suspiciously, which made her giggle again. She lifted her hands, palms up, in an innocent gesture, the grin growing wide on her face. Slowly, she shook her head, as if she had no idea why he stared so. His mouth twisted and he narrowed his eyes as if he knew exactly what she'd been thinking.

"Hey! You did that on purpose!"

The lighthearted moment broken, Darcy darted a glance along the fence. Herbert, his face tomato red, glowered at Joel. "You meant to sling whitewash on me." He used his sleeve to wipe the offending streak from his jaw.

"Did not!"

"Did so!"

"Boys!" Brent came up behind them. "What's going on here?"

"He meant to do it, Mr. Thomas."

Joel crossed his arms, apparently forgetting he still held a wet paintbrush. "You can't prove it," he said, a smirk on his face. "It was an accident, pure and simple."

Darcy wondered why a little more whitewash should matter to Herbert, who was already spattered with white, but she kept silent.

"It weren't no accident!" Herbert's eyes narrowed. "It was about as much an accident as you stopping up the stovepipe with—"

"Shut up!" Joel growled and uncrossed his arms, all indifference gone.

Herbert's expression was smug. "That's why the stove didn't work right last winter, Mr. Thomas. 'Cause Joel took some old rags and climbed the roof—"

With a ferocious yell, Joel barreled into Herbert, tackling him to the ground. "You squealer! I'll show you not to double-cross me. You're just as much to blame for holding the ladder."

Joel straddled Herbert and lifted the hand holding the paint-brush high. Before Brent could intervene, Joel gave the boy's face a few quick swipes with the brush, covering Herbert's red skin with white until he resembled a ghost. "There, have some more!"

"Aggghhh!" Herbert's hands went to his face. "He got it in my eyes! I can't see!"

"Mercy! What's going on now?" Irma screeched as she ran from the kitchen door, raising her skirts high. "Joel, you stop that this minute!"

Brent now had both arms around Joel, who still swung the paintbrush like a weapon, and pulled him back. Herbert lay on the ground, howling, hands over his eyes. Michael, his great size making him awkward, ran from overseeing the boys at the end of the row. He lifted the injured boy off the ground and jogged to the house.

"Irma, call Doc Sanderson," Brent ordered through clenched teeth as he restrained a struggling Joel. "Miss Evans, wash Herbert's eyes out." He looked at the other boys, and Darcy noticed his glasses were missing. "The contest is canceled."

Ignoring the cries of disappointment, Darcy ran after Michael, her heart beating with misgiving. Once inside the house, she pumped water into a basin. In the hallway, Irma cranked the telephone, trying to get the operator. She spoke into the mouthpiece on the wooden box attached to the wall. "Hello, Miranda? Miranda, can you hear me? Get Doc to the Refuge as soon as possible. One of the boys is hurt."

Darcy stared into the filled basin. *Lord, help me. Don't let this poor boy go blind. Show me what to do.* She positioned the crying Herbert, placing his upper body over the table and turning his head sideways. Dipping a cup in the water, she saw she would need another pair of hands and glanced at Michael. "I could use assistance." Her voice wavered with the doubt she felt.

"Of course, Lass." His expression grave, Michael took hold of Herbert's small wrists, forcing the boy's curled fingers from his face, and held them in one massive hand. With his other hand, Michael held the boy's head steady.

Using her thumb and forefinger, Darcy opened his tightly clenched eyelid and trickled water into the corner of his eye. Herbert howled in pain, but she didn't stop. Instead, she repeated the process several times with both eyes. Her heart wrenched at his pitiful sobs.

When the sound of horses' hooves and the jangle of harness finally came, Darcy felt a sudden relief, knowing someone more qualified would soon be taking over. Portly Doc Sanderson bustled into the kitchen. He quickly surveyed the scene, his full lips thinning. "Take the boy into the parlor, Michael. Put him on the sofa. I'll examine him there."

Michael carried Herbert into the next room, and Doc followed. Darcy collapsed onto the vacated chair and propped her elbows on the wet table. She dropped her forehead onto her palms. "Help him, Lord. Take care of his eyes."

"Amen," Irma murmured. "I'll make coffee." The clang of metal hitting metal rang through the air while she went about her task.

Darcy eyed the water that had run off the edge of the table to form a puddle on the planks. "I'll take care of this mess."

As she put away the mop, the back door opened and Brent walked inside. His suit jacket was covered with white smears and speckles, his hair was disheveled, and his glasses were missing. Never had Darcy seen the proper schoolmaster in such a state. She propped the mop against the wall. "What happened to your spectacles?"

Without a word, he fished them from his coat pocket. A wire earpiece had broken off, and a crack zigzagged over one lens.

Darcy peered up at him sheepishly. "Er, sorry, Guv'ner. Why don't you sit down and rest a spell? Irma's makin' coffee."

His sober countenance melted into one of relief. "Coffee sounds superb." He took a seat opposite Darcy. "How is the boy?"

"Doc's with him in the parlor."

Brent nodded, his gaze pensive as he studied his hands clasped on the table. Irma set down two steaming cups of coffee and followed it with two plates, each containing a thick slice of blackberry pie. "No sense letting it go to waste," she muttered.

Darcy stared at the dessert she'd made only this morning. The purplish black berries and sauce oozed from beneath a thin, flaky crust. A prize for the winner. What a farce that had turned out to be!

Darcy pushed away her plate, unable to enjoy the treat. Brent, apparently, had no such compunction; and Darcy watched as he lifted a forkful of the fragrant pie to his mouth.

"Ah, Miss Evans, you've outdone yourself," he said after he chewed and swallowed the first bite. He drank the rest of his coffee. "Irma, may I have another cup?"

Irma let Darcy know from the start that she preferred to be known simply as "Irma," and Darcy assumed that was why Brent called the cook by her Christian name.

"It's a crying shame about your suit." Irma tsk-tsked. "Not sure I can get whitewash out, being how it's got lime and whiting in it, but I can give it a try."

"Thank you. I appreciate the offer. However, I think such an attempt would prove futile." Brent gave Irma a faded smile and held out a sleeve. "The paint appears to have absorbed into the wool and dried. I've needed to acquire a new suit for some time, and I suppose now is the time to do so."

"You can have what's left of my eight dollars," Darcy blurted. "I still have a little over four dollars left."

Brent's eyes widened. "I can't take your money, Miss Evans."

"Whyever not?"

The question seemed to baffle him. "Because it's yours."

"Well, now, I know that. I'm offering it. All, or as much as you need." She lowered her gaze to her untouched pie. "I'm feelin' a mite guilty—bein' as how the contest was my idea. And you'll need new glasses." Uncomfortable, she took a sip of the bitter black brew, trying not to scowl and hurt Irma's feelings. She really didn't like coffee.

"I appreciate your generous offer." Brent's voice came more quietly. "But I do have adequate funds to obtain a suit. I keep a spare pair of eyeglasses in my bureau drawer, as well."

Darcy gave a swift nod but didn't look up. She took another sip of coffee.

"Well, I need to be seeing what Charleigh wants for her lunch," Irma said, bustling from the room.

Brent picked up his cup. "Don't feel too badly, Miss Evans. Everyone is entitled to a substandard idea once in a lifetime. It's part of being human."

Her gaze shot upward. "Substandard?"

"A bad idea." When she shook her head in confusion, he added, "The contest."

"Oh, but I don't think my idea a bad one."

His sympathetic expression changed to one of incredulity. "Surely you must be jesting."

"No, Guv'ner." Her voice came steady, and she carefully set her cup on the saucer. "Herbert and Joel are always bickering.

Why should all the lads be punished for the mischief of two boys?"

His cup hit the saucer with a harsh clink. "Miss Evans—"

"Hear me out, Guv'ner. What happened today isn't so unusual, though 'tis a pity the scuffle ended with Herbert injured." Concern washed over her again as she turned her gaze toward the closed door that led to the parlor. "But Herbert is always gettin' hurt, and Joel is always fighting—usually Herbert. You can hardly blame the contest for what happened today."

He released a weary sigh. "Granted, you may be right. Yet what do you propose we do to prevent this problem from resurfacing in the future?"

She shrugged one shoulder. "Simple. Because of their behavior, Joel and Herbert are excluded from the next contest. Tomorrow is Saturday. We'll try again then."

Exasperation filled Brent's eyes. "Miss Evans, did anyone ever tell you that you are one obdurate woman?"

"Obdurate?"

"Stubborn."

Darcy smiled. "And did anyone ever tell you, Guv'ner, that you have the nicest blue eyes? Bright as robins' eggs they are, clear and shiny. You really should go without your glasses more often. It would be nice to see your eyes without them spectacles always in the way."

A flush of red swept up his neck to his face. Darcy thought it a good thing that his mouth wasn't full of dessert. She studied his face and form, thinking him to be quite attractive all the way around. *If only. . .*

"Eat your pie, Guv'ner. Things are quite simpler than you're makin' 'em out to be. You'll see. One day, hopefully, you'll see everything that's sittin' in front of your face—with or without the aid of your spectacles."

Brent recovered enough to blot his mouth with a napkin. "And just what is that convoluted piece of logic supposed to mean?"

"Just this. Pigeons might not be as beautiful as peacocks, or as graceful as swans, or sing as pretty as larks—but they have their place in this world too." She stood, braced her hands on the table, and leaned toward him. "And you know what, Guv'ner? Some people prefer spendin' time with the likes o' them than with the other high falutin birds."

Darcy flounced from the room, leaving Brent gaping after her in bewilderment.

# seven

After filling out quarterly progress reports, Brent decided it was time for a break. He stood, stretched the kinks out from between his shoulder blades, and glanced out the window overlooking the front yard. His brows rose in surprise.

Golden sunlight dappled bright circles through the sparsely leafed branches and onto Joel's white blond hair. He sat under an oak, his arms wrapped around his legs, his face on his knees. A trickle of red and gold fell around him as several leaves in the branches above surrendered their posts and wearily drifted to the ground.

Brent puzzled a moment and then headed for the door. Once outside, he made his way to where the boy sat, his crunching footsteps announcing his approach. Joel lifted his face, his tear-smudged cheeks evidence he'd been crying. His bright eyes were defiant. "What do you want?" His voice came out harsh.

Brent decided now was not the time to reprimand the boy for disrespect. Without being asked, he awkwardly sank to the leafy ground beside him and looped his arms around his bent knees, matching Joel's stance. Brent's everyday suit coat had been ruined from the whitewashing experience, so there was no need to protect it. He would replace it the next time he went into town.

He stared at the silvery blue horizon beyond the pasture, where two cows and four horses grazed on what was left of the grass. "Days like this often cause me to ponder former episodes of my life," Brent said quietly. From the corner of his eye, he could tell he'd won Joel's attention.

"Yeah. So?" Suspicion laced the boy's voice.

"Autumn is a season of change," Brent replied, still not looking at the lad. "A time when some things must die, so that they may be reborn."

"That's silly." Joel swiped a hand underneath his nose. "Why should something have to die so's it can be reborn? Why can't it just go on living forever?"

"Well, I believe that was the original plan, Joel." He plucked up a withered brown leaf. "Observe this leaf. Once it was green and soft and shiny. Now look at it." Brent crushed it in his hand. It crackled into small particles, showering like dust to the ground. "People can be like that. They can allow hatred and bitterness to make them hard and dry and brittle and age them before their time."

The boy said nothing, only stared at the brown fragments.

"What happens when spring comes, Joel?"

Indignant blue eyes snapped upward. "Any moron can tell you that, Mr. Thomas—and I ain't no moron."

Brent nodded. "Actually you're quite smart when you put your mind to it. Yet suppose you enlighten me in any case."

Joel rolled his eyes. "The trees get new leaves on 'em."

"Exactly! Brand-new leaves—shiny and green. But first the leaves start as tiny buds."

"So?" Joel shrugged, clearly bored.

"So, that's what happens when a person asks Jesus to be his Savior." Brent scooped up the brown fragments. "We're like this before having Jesus. Old, dry, dead in our sins. When we ask God to come inside our hearts, He gives us new life—and a new start. Like a bud in springtime. As we grow with Him, we bloom until we reach our full potential, though as long as we're on this earth, He constantly will be perfecting us."

Joel eyed the crisp foliage. "So what did these ole leaves do to deserve to die? Did they sin?"

Brent let out an exasperated breath. "You're missing the point, Joel. These are merely leaves. They don't have spirits like you and I do. Every person needs Jesus to be reborn. I was using the leaves to illustrate that."

Joel raised his chin. "My father never needed Jesus. So why should I?"

"And where is your father now?"

Joel's expression grew even more belligerent. "You know where he is. But he's only in jail 'cause someone double-crossed him!"

Brent paused before responding, not wanting to alienate the boy further. He knew Joel held his father in high regard, despite the man's lengthy criminal record. He was the boy's father, after all.

"The bad things we do have consequences, Joel; remember that. If you allow God into your life, He'll teach you a better way, a way without sin. Sin leads to prison. If not an actual prison with bars that you can see, then a prison of the heart that you can't see. People can have invisible bars across their heart without even realizing it. And that prison door keeps God out. They have to *choose* to let Jesus use the key and open the door to set them free. Yet many don't."

"That's silly." Joel scowled. "Why would anyone want to stay in some ole prison?"

"Perhaps due to fear of change?" Brent shrugged. "I really don't know if there's one particular answer to that question. There are probably many. Yet the most important question you need to consider, Joel, is this: What is your reason for staying in your heart prison?"

Joel's gaze lowered. The whir of insects seemed to grow louder as the quiet intensified between them. From across the pasture, a cow lowed. The boy continued to stare at the dead leaves, his mouth drawn into a tight line.

After minutes of silence, Brent stood, knowing he should return to the study and his unfinished work. He hoped he'd made some sort of impact but doubted it from the glower on Joel's face. He turned to go.

"Mr. Thomas?"

Brent looked back. The boy's eyes were again forlorn.

"I didn't mean to make Herbert go blind." Tears strained Joel's voice. "He shouldn't have squealed—but I never meant to hurt him. Not really."

"I realize that, Joel. We won't know if there's permanent damage to Herbert's vision until the doctor removes the bandages. Actually, Dr. Sanderson was quite optimistic of Herbert's prognosis, due to the eye rinses and salves that were administered."

Joel stared down at his shoes. "Do you think Herbert will ever talk to me again?" His lower teeth slid along his upper lip. "I mean, do you think he'll forgive me?"

"There's only one way to find out."

Joel looked up in surprise. "You mean ask him?"

"Yes."

"But what if he don't want nothin' to do with me no more? What if he hates me now?"

Brent regarded the boy. "Would you like to know what I really think?" At his slight nod, Brent continued. "I think the combination of the words *what* and *if* never should have been introduced to the English language. Those two words hold people back and often produce unnecessary fear. The past can't be altered, Joel, but the future can."

The boy pursed his lips in thought. "Meaning I should go and find out for myself, huh?"

"That would be a wise choice. I'll accompany you, if you'd prefer."

Joel hesitated another few seconds, then shook his head. "Thanks all the same, Mr. Thomas, but I best do this alone."

❧

Darcy sat in a chair next to the sofa and read to Herbert, who lay snug underneath a blanket. A long strip of cotton padding was wrapped around his head, over his eyes. For three days, the helpless patient had been pampered, read to, and waited on hand and foot.

Irma also felt sorry for the lad, worried he might be blinded for life, and constantly baked him goodies. From her room upstairs, Charleigh had ordered that Herbert not be moved from the parlor; and the sofa was loaded with blankets to make a comfortable bed, a fire ever-present in the grate to warm him.

A few of the boys had visited the patient, and Tommy gave Herbert half his winnings from the contest—a second blackberry pie Darcy had made. Though Tommy's walk was hampered because of his clubfoot, he made up for any lack with his strong arms, which had worked rapidly to paint the fence.

Darcy finished the third chapter from *Robinson Crusoe* and closed the book. "That's enough for today."

"Awww, don't quit. Read more, Miss Darcy."

"One chapter is enough. My voice is tired."

"But you left off right at the good part!"

Darcy ignored his plea, since he said that about every chapter she read. "How about some cider?" She rose and set the book on the table.

"Don't want no cider." Herbert pouted and crossed his arms. "Want *Robinson Crusoe*."

"Herbert," she said in warning, her hands going to her hips. A movement near the entryway caught her eye, and Joel walked into the room. Brent stood behind him, next to the wall.

The boy's eyes were uncertain as he stared at Herbert. At the hesitant shushing of footsteps on carpet, Herbert's head lifted higher. "Who's there, Miss Darcy?"

Darcy opened her mouth to answer but stopped when Brent shook his head and put a forefinger to his lips. He crooked his finger for her to join him and disappeared around the corner.

She turned to Herbert. "I'll be back with some tea and cheese sandwiches later."

"Don't want no cheese. Want thick slices of ham."

Darcy grimaced at Herbert's pigheadedness. She refused to explain to Herbert for the fifth time that they had run out of those items and needed to replenish the larder. He was set on being obstinate today, and the constant pampering he received did him no good, in her opinion. Yet she'd been just as much at fault.

Darcy strode from the room, watching curiously as Joel moved toward the sofa. When she came alongside Brent, Darcy turned in the direction of the kitchen. Surprise shot through her when he grasped her elbow to stop her. He gave a short shake of his head, pulling her awkwardly to stand in front of him. Her shoulder blades brushed his chest.

"I know it's wrong to eavesdrop," he whispered near her ear, "but in this case I'm making an exception. I'll explain later."

Darcy's heart somersaulted at the feel of his warm breath on her neck, stirring her hair. Afraid to move—even to breathe—for fear he would remove his hand from her arm and step away, she remained as motionless as a wooden hat tree while they peeked around the corner.

"Who's there, I said?" Herbert pushed himself to a sitting position on the couch.

"It's me. Joel."

Herbert didn't say a word.

"I, uh, just wanted to see how you're doing."

"Whadda you care?" Herbert sneered.

Brent tensed and his hold on Darcy's elbow tightened. He pressed closer to hear, his chest now flat against her back. She swallowed over a dry throat.

Joel seemed stymied for words. "I. . .uh. . ."

"Just get out." Herbert turned his bandaged head away.

Instead of being cowed by the harsh words, Joel stood taller. "You shoulda never double-crossed me, Herbert. I don't like squealers. That's why I painted your face. But I sure never meant to hurt your eyes none. I was just trying to shut up your mouth." His arms crossed in defiance. "And that's all I'm ever gonna say about it. So if it ain't good enough—well, that's just too bad!"

Darcy felt Brent's chest rise and fall and heard a weary sigh escape. Again his warm breath fanned her neck, sending her heart into another spasm. The steady crackle of fire in the grate filled the eternal moment of silence in the room.

Herbert's head turned Joel's way. "Ever read *Robinson Crusoe?*"

"No." Joel walked the few feet to the chair Darcy had vacated and picked up the book from the table, eyeing the cover. "Is it one of them sissified books of Miss Charleigh's?"

"Naw—I wouldn't have nothin' to do with them kinds of books—you know that. It's about a man who gets shipwrecked on a desert island," Herbert said, excitement tingeing his voice. "Miss Darcy's reading it to me, though she's sure takin' her sweet time about doin' it!"

Darcy heard Brent quietly chuckle, his chest vibrating with the motion.

"No foolin'? A desert island? With pirates and buried treasure and wild animals eating people?"

"Not exactly. Leastways nothin' like that's happened yet. But he's all alone, and it's an adventure just the same."

Brent moved away, gently pulling Darcy with him. He headed toward the kitchen, and she fell into step beside him. "What was that all about?" Darcy still felt a bit topsy-turvy from his recent closeness, and her voice came out funny.

"A successful lesson on the importance of contrition and forgiveness. Though the apology left much to be desired," Brent added wryly. "Still, I think it achieved its purpose."

He turned his head, smiling. "This calls for a victory celebration. Assuming they're still there, would you care to join me in partaking of the last two pieces of blackberry pie and coffee—or tea if you prefer?"

Darcy nodded, knowing she would join him for a trip around the world in a hot air balloon had he asked.

"Together, Miss Evans, I think we can do this." His words came out confident.

Her breath caught in her throat at the word *together*. "Do what, Guv'ner?"

"Steer the boys in Stewart and Charleigh's absence. I believe we finally have reached an understanding and will begin to see some positive results for all our hard labor." He paused. "Perhaps the time has come to present the plan."

"Plan?"

"The carnival. It might be just the incentive the boys need to continue along the road to improvement. The outing would be a desirable goal, one that will help them strive to succeed and recognize that life can bring rewards for making correct choices. . . ."

Darcy smiled as she listened to Brent talk as though he'd always approved of her plan.

There just might be hope for him yet.

&

"How are you feeling? Better?" Darcy plunked down on the chenille spread at the end of Charleigh's bed.

"Merely bored," Charleigh said. "You have no idea how difficult it is to stay in bed! And I still have two months to go."

Her gaze turned to the sepia photo of her husband in its silver frame. "But I'm thankful I've carried the baby this long, and I certainly don't mean to sound as if I'm complaining. Still, I wish I'd get another letter. I think he's avoiding me. His letters have been so impersonal lately. Though at least he's writing, so that's something. He never was much of a letter-writer, both during my last two years at Turreney Farm and during the war."

"Have you written him about the baby?"

Charleigh lowered her gaze to the blanket and shook her head.

"Honestly! Don't you think he might begin to wonder when he comes home and finds you with a child in your arms? Assuming he stays away that long, of course."

"It's not exactly something you can dash off in a letter, Darcy. 'Dear Stewart, everyone's fine. The school is running smoothly, the progress reports are in order—oh, and by the way, I'm seven months with child.' I just couldn't do it. Especially in something as impersonal as a letter. Besides, I don't want to get his hopes up if. . .if something should happen."

"Now, I'll hear no more of that kind of talk!"

Charleigh sobered. Penitent for her harsh words, Darcy leaned over to lay her hand on Charleigh's. "You have to hold on, Luv. Even Doc Sanderson is optimistic with the way things are going."

"He did seem positive during his last visit, didn't he?" Charleigh asked, hope in her eyes.

"Yes, he did. And never you mind about Stewart. More the surprise for him—and another thing you can look forward to seeing. The look on his face when he finds out. Ought to be about as good as when Brent's mouth drops open after I say something shocking. Though I certainly don't do such a thing on purpose." Darcy winked, eliciting a giggle from Charleigh.

A short knock at the door was followed by Alice Larkin. "Hope I'm not intruding," she said uncertainly. Her salt-and-pepper hair had been swept under a kerchief. Obviously she'd been doing housework. A pair of silver-rimmed spectacles perched at the end of her thin nose. Darcy knew that Alice used to be Michael's housekeeper before they discovered a mutual respect and liking for one another, though Charleigh once mentioned that she suspected Alice had always loved her father.

Charleigh smiled at her stepmother. "Come in. We were just discussing how surprised Stewart will be when he learns he's a father."

Alice set a canvas bag on the foot of the bed. "That he will, make no mistake about it. I still can't understand why you didn't tell him before he left. Though it's none of my business, I suppose," she muttered. Her thin lips stretched into a smile. "And have you given any thought as to what the child will be wearing when he makes his entrance into the world?"

Charleigh's forehead creased. "Wearing?"

Alice shook her head. "If it wasn't for me, that poor babe would likely be stark naked throughout his entire infancy." She pulled a large skein of ivory-colored yarn from her bag, followed by a pair of bone knitting needles.

Charleigh looked at the materials, then up at her stepmother.

Alice lifted her brows. "Well, what are you gawking at, Charleigh?"

"I don't know how to knit."

"And what do you think I'm here for? I'm aiming to teach you. The good Lord knows you need something useful to do, stuck in this bed day in and day out."

Darcy could have hugged the old woman for her thoughtfulness. "What a wonderful idea!" Another thought occurred to her. "If it wouldn't be too much trouble, could you teach me too?"

Alice smiled. "Got someone special in mind you want to make something for, Missy?"

Heat rushed to Darcy's face at Alice's astute gaze. "Just wantin' to learn is all."

"Well, I expect it shouldn't be too hard coughing up another pair of knitting needles."

Charleigh leaned forward and fingered the ivory-colored yarn. For the first time since Alice came into the room, she gave a genuine smile.

A short knock sounded, and Irma poked her head inside. "Darcy? Sorry to interrupt, but I need to be talking tonight's menu over with you. What do you think of having baked salmon again, with cooked peas and carrots? I ran out of asparagus, though I'm sure the boys wouldn't mind hearing that piece o' news."

"That sounds fine, Irma. I'll be down to help in a little while." Darcy still worked as Cook's assistant; though since she'd taken over Charleigh's role of running things, Irma now often sought Darcy's approval on meals.

Once the cook left, Alice showed Charleigh and Darcy how to hold the needles. She pulled a long string of yarn from the skein, preparing to give the first lesson.

Uneven footsteps came along the hallway, followed by a hesitant knock.

"Yes?" Charleigh called.

The glass doorknob turned. "Miss Darcy?" Tommy said through the crack in the door. "Herbert wants to know if you'll read him another chapter from that island book."

Darcy rolled her eyes toward the ceiling. Every day Herbert

asked the same thing. "Tell him he'll have to wait 'til tomorrow. Have ye finished your lessons?"

"Yes'm. I'll tell Herbert what you said." The door clicked closed, and awkward shuffling and clomping faded as Tommy limped away.

Darcy grinned. Since the boys had been in competition for the carnival this past week, no one had to push them to study.

"That Herbert is getting downright spoiled," Alice said to nobody in particular.

Darcy chose not to comment, especially since Alice was right.

"Now, as I was saying, you loop this piece around the tip of the needle, like so—"

A loud rap sounded on the door, shaking the wood in its casing.

Alice heaved a loud sigh. "It's getting to be about as popular in here as Grand Central!"

"Come in," Charleigh said, raising her voice.

Chris's head popped through this time. "Miss Darcy?"

"Yes, Chris, what is it?"

"Mr. Thomas wants to speak with you in the study."

Darcy rose from the bed. "I better go see what he wants."

Ignoring the shrewd gleam in Alice's eyes, Darcy swept past her and downstairs. She found Brent in Stewart's oak-paneled study. Brent sat in a chair behind the desk where he took care of the bookwork in Stewart's absence. He toyed with an envelope, staring at it as though his mind were a thousand miles away. His lips were turned down at the corners.

Darcy waited what seemed an interminable amount of time for him to notice her. She cleared her throat loudly.

"Hmmm?" Brent looked up, his eyes vacant. Seeing her on the threshold, he straightened. "Miss Evans—please, come in. Close the door and have a seat."

Curious, Darcy did as requested, then moved across the faded carpet to the chair across from Brent's. He regarded her soberly. "I must make a trip into town this weekend. I'll need you to take care of things in my absence." He didn't sound too happy about the prospect.

"Trouble?"

Brent's gaze shifted back to the envelope. He didn't answer right away. "My brother. He's coming to town and wishes to speak with me."

Darcy nodded as if she understood, though she was confused. Studying his unhappy expression, she ventured, "And is this a bad thing, Guv'ner—him wishin' to speak with you?"

His gaze again lifted to hers, his expression weary. "With Bill, Miss Evans, it's always a bad thing."

Before she could think twice, she was out of her chair and around to his side of the desk. Kneeling in front of him, she put her hand over his in encouragement. "Well, then, Guv'ner, I believe prayer is what's needed here, instead of you mopin' about the situation. Don't you? I'll pray with ye, if ye'd like."

Dumbly, he nodded, his eyes wide behind the spectacles. Bowing her head, her hand still cupped over his warm one, she murmured a heartfelt prayer for the brothers' reunion and God's leading in it all.

When Darcy finished, she looked up. Brent's eyes shimmered softly with something akin to amazement. Yet he said nothing. Was he so shocked by her behavior?

Suddenly uneasy, Darcy rose, made an excuse that she needed to help Irma with the meal, and left the room. She supposed she shouldn't have been so forward. Yet she hoped Brent didn't mind her praying with him. In fact, she hoped it was only the beginning of such occurrences.

# eight

At half past two, Brent paced the station's loading area and peered off to the west. No pillar of gray smoke loomed above the trees nor marred the gray-blue sky to announce the train's arrival. No monstrous roar of clacking wheels shook the rails. No haunting blast of a sirenlike whistle pierced the still air. Again he glanced at his pocket watch. It wasn't usual for the train to arrive even a few minutes late. Unless it wasn't the train that was tardy, but his watch that was running slow. He lifted the timepiece to his ear. Not hearing any ticking, he shook it.

"Prompt as usual, little brother."

Almost dropping the watch, Brent tensed at the jocular words coming from behind him and pivoted to look. Bill stood only feet away, dapper in a silk suit with broad pinstripes. A matching gray felt fedora with a black band topped his hair, which was slicked down and looked a shade darker than its usual wheat blond color. No common bowler for his brother! Even his black Oxfords appeared shiny and new. Obviously life hadn't treated his brother too harshly, although the lines bracketing his mouth and the faint furrows between his brows testified that this wasn't entirely the case. Identical in features and coloring, the similarities between the brothers ended there.

"Bill." Brent nodded curtly, wishing he'd given in to the need to replace his suit coat. He pocketed his watch and cupped a hand over one elbow to hide an offending streak of dried whitewash. Such a gesture was futile when he thought about it. White speckles dotted the entire coat. "Where did you come from? The train hasn't arrived."

"I decided to take an earlier one. I came into town yesterday and stayed the night at the hotel."

"Yesterday? Why didn't you ring me at the reformatory?"

"Let's just say I thought the fewer people who knew my whereabouts, the better." Bill threw him one of his dashing smiles, one that Brent knew the women swooned over. "I decided a discreet and *expeditious* entrance into your small town would be the best plan for all concerned."

Brent ignored the mocking way Bill stressed the word. His brother always poked fun at Brent's thirst for knowledge and use of elaborate words. "So, what brings you to our unexciting little town? Are matters getting uncomfortable in the big city? Is the law too close for comfort?"

Bill chuckled. "You know, that's what I love about you, little brother. You always know how to make a guy feel welcome."

Brent refrained from answering. The last time Bill sought him out had been for monetary purposes. Judging from his brother's suave appearance, Brent didn't think that was the case this time.

The stationmaster ambled out onto the platform and gave them a cursory once-over before peering toward the west, where the faint roar of the oncoming train could now be heard.

"Let's take this elsewhere," Bill muttered, cocking the brim of his hat low over his forehead. "I don't have much time."

"I have a wagon parked around the side of the building."

"Doesn't surprise me. You never were one for progress."

Brent chose to ignore the barb and moved in the direction of the horse and cart, with Bill following. Once they'd taken their place on the long bench seat, Brent flicked the reins. Polly tossed her dark mane and plodded down the dirt road. Bill grew unusually quiet and stared at the long line of storefronts.

Brent cleared his throat. "Mind telling me where we're going?"

"Nowhere. Anywhere. Just drive."

Brent sighed, tamping down his irritation. When they

reached the lane leading to the road out of town, Brent took it. Slender trees on both sides of the narrow path formed a brown latticework canopy of bare limbs above their heads. Winter's bite sharpened the chill air, and Brent was relieved that the contest winners for the carnival would be announced soon. On second thought, a good snowfall might prevent the event from taking place. So perhaps he should pray for snow instead.

It had been alarming to discover that Joel was tied with an intelligent but forgetful boy named Frank as one of the three who would achieve the right to attend the event. A week remained, and a major test involving geography still needed to be taken. Brent had to admit Darcy's plan was working well— all of the boys exhibited their best behavior. Still, the prospect of taking them to a carnival made him uneasy.

"I suppose you're wondering why I asked to see you." Bill's voice startled Brent from his reverie.

"The thought had crossed my mind."

"Okay, it's like this—I've decided to embark on a seagoing career. Ships are always in need of a few able-bodied sailors, and I've applied for the job."

Brent almost dropped the reins. "You're making sport of me again, aren't you?"

"Not this time."

Brent stared at his impeccably dressed brother, who'd always had a penchant for the finer things in life. He couldn't imagine this man in a drab, ill-fitting uniform, eating food of non-descriptive taste, while bouncing along five-foot waves. Certainly his brother was joshing him.

"You're right about there being trouble—only not with the law this time. That I could handle." Bill released a weary sigh. "Let's just say it's no longer safe to be connected with the men of my association, not after what I accidentally stumbled upon. And that's all I can tell you. It's for your own good, so don't look at me that way. I just thought you should know what's what, in case you don't hear from me for several years."

*Several years?* "I take it your acquaintances aren't aware of your plans?"

"I left without saying good-bye, if that's what you mean." Bill's mouth twisted into a wry grin. "I found it far safer for my continued health."

Brent mulled over his brother's words. He knew from previous newspaper accounts that the tough group of men Bill associated with wasn't above murder. "Do you plan to inform our parents of your decision?" Brent asked quietly.

"I thought I'd leave that up to you. They probably wouldn't care one way or the other what happens to me and would be relieved to hear they were rid of their black-hearted son."

Brent drew his brows together. Despite all the trouble Bill had caused, he was still family. As small boys, they had been inseparable. What had happened to change that?

Anxiety blurred Brent's focus of the surroundings but sharpened his imagination. "What if they discover your whereabouts? What happens then?" He wasn't sure why he voiced the questions since the answers were obvious, given Bill's previous statement.

"Let's just say I'd sink with the anchor—permanently."

"I don't find that amusing."

Bill looked at him, his mouth and eyes wide in feigned surprise. "Do I detect a note of concern, little brother?"

Brent's lips thinned. "Will you kindly desist with the sarcasm? For once, try to be serious when the situation warrants it."

Bill released a loud breath, discernible even over the clopping of horse's hooves on hard-packed soil. "Serious. All right. Frankly, I don't want to consider the possibility. My odds for staying alive are good, I think. There was another man once—Phil something or other. I can't remember his last name. He joined up with us years ago, but was only around a short time. . .Rawlins. Yes—Phil Rawlins. That was it. He was great in his line of work—a con man and safecracker—but untrustworthy as they come. When word leaked out that my former associates were planning to do him in, he slipped away and wasn't heard from again. I can do the same."

"How do you know they didn't find him and kill him?"

Bill smiled, though his eyes were deadly serious. "Believe me, Brent. If they'd rubbed him out, it wouldn't have been kept a secret. Not among those men."

Brent closed his eyes. "Bill, answer me this. Have you, yourself, ever killed anyone?"

A short silence ensued. "It might be best not to ask questions you really don't want the answers to, little brother." This time when Bill spoke, his voice was grave and not in any way amused.

Clenching his jaw, Brent gave a brisk nod.

"You better head back to the station. I've told you all you need to know, and I have a train to catch. The ship I've signed on with leaves at morning's tide." Bill threw Brent a crooked smile. "I sound like a sailor already, don't I?"

*Hardly,* Brent thought, but didn't say it.

"I've heard a bit of gambling goes on aboard ship—with or without the captain's knowledge. Lady Luck and I have always been soul mates. I doubt I'll have a problem finding my place with the boys." He winked.

The ride back was quiet, and Brent relived the conversation in his mind. Didn't even a morsel of decency remain in his brother? Was he truly a lost cause as their mother had once stated?

When they pulled up to the station, Brent faced Bill. "For what it's worth, I want you to know I'm praying for you. I have been for a long time. You're still my brother, regardless of everything. God keep you safe." He held out his hand.

Bill studied it a moment, then looked up at Brent in surprised confusion. After a short time, he took his brother's hand in a firm shake. "You know, Brent, sometimes I really do wish things could have turned out differently." He paused as if he wanted to say more, then seemed to change his mind and jumped down from the wagon.

His jovial manner returned. "You may have always been something of a fuddy-duddy, but you're an okay guy in my book, little brother." Tipping his hat, he offered Brent one last devil-may-care grin. "Don't take any wooden nickels!"

Brent shook his head as he watched him jog to the platform. Bill was the one running for his life due to wrong choices, and he was telling *Brent* not to do anything stupid? Deep concern for his brother's welfare engulfed him. The righteous anger and betrayal Brent felt when Bill's nefarious actions caused him to be ostracized as a schoolmaster had at some point melted away without his realizing it.

"Keep safe, big brother," Brent said under his breath as he watched Bill disappear around the corner. "Dear Lord, keep him safe. Help him to find You. Send perfect laborers into his path, people to whom he would listen. In fact, as muleheaded as he is, perhaps an episode with a burning bush might prove more beneficial."

He grinned at the thought of such a meeting.

❧

Darcy counted her remaining prize money from the poetry contest. Whatever should she do with it? She'd bought all she wanted. Charleigh didn't seem to need it or want it, for that matter. And Darcy didn't think she should single out any of the boys for fear of causing rivalries among them.

Hearing a horse, she moved to her attic window and looked down. Brent drove the wagon through the gates, along the lane toward the barn. Chickens squawked, scattering from the path. Darcy's first thought of why the chickens were running loose and not in their pen was followed by the shock of seeing Brent in a new suit—a warm golden brown one, classically styled.

She ran down the stairs and out the door. With lifted skirts, she ran to the barn. The chickens gave loud protests, skittering out of her way.

Brent climbed down from the wagon and faced her in the shade of the barn's overhang. The suit was good for his eyes and skin tone—much better than the drab color he'd worn before.

"You bought a new suit," Darcy blurted when she could catch her breath.

Brent cast a disparaging glance at his clothes. "The tailor made this two weeks ago. The previous customer was unable to pay for it after ordering alterations. Surprisingly, it fit, though it's not something I would have picked under normal circumstances. Yet I could no longer wear that paint-speckled suit. Here at the reform it wasn't so bad, but in town, to do so was embarrassing."

"Well, I like it," Darcy said with a decisive nod. "It does something for you. Makes you look less stuffy."

The corners of Brent's mouth turned down at the compliment-gone-wrong, and Darcy quickly changed the subject. "How did the chat with your brother go?"

"He's decided to become a sailor and is going to sea."

Darcy wasn't sure how to reply. She thought Brent should be pleased that his brother had left the criminal life. Yet he looked far from happy.

Brent stared at the black-feathered hen that strutted and pecked at the ground near his shoes. "Why are the chickens running loose? Who has the job of tending them this week?"

Darcy thought a moment. "Frank," she said hesitantly.

They stared somberly at one another. Frank was tied with Joel as the third boy to go to the carnival. Because of Frank's negligence, there was no longer a tie.

"Miss Evans, it wouldn't be wise to allow Joel to attend the carnival," Brent said as though reading her mind. "On the outside he's shown an aptitude to change. However, I don't think we're observing a genuine change of heart, as the other boys seem to have had. To put it bluntly, I don't trust Joel and don't want the responsibility involved in taking him away from the Refuge."

Darcy chewed on her lower lip. She didn't trust the boy either. There was something about the look in his eyes when she would suddenly turn and catch him watching her. As if he were waiting for a certain moment—though to do what, Darcy had no idea.

"Then what'll we do, Guv'ner? We can't change the rules this late in the game. We'd look dishonest—promising the boys one thing and then not living up to our part of the bargain."

"I didn't say that the decision would apply to all the boys. Only to Joel."

"I understand," Darcy said impatiently. "But if we did such a thing, the others would think we don't stand by our word. Maybe it wouldn't affect them directly this time, but they'd remember what we did, sure as I'm standin' here. And we may wind up with discipline problems because of it."

Obviously upset, Brent pulled off his glasses and cleaned the spotless lenses with his handkerchief. "Had I known Joel would catch up to the others, I might not have agreed to the idea. I sincerely didn't believe he would win. You and I both know that Joel is just waiting for an opportunity to run. He talks incessantly of finding his father. Suppose he decides to escape while we're at the carnival? What then?"

"Michael will be with us," Darcy countered. "The boys know better than to act up with him around."

"Yet suppose that doesn't prove to be the case when Joel's in a public, unrestricted area? Suppose the lure of freedom proves too powerful for him?"

Darcy put her fists on her hips. "As for supposin', suppose the sky falls down around our ears like it did for Chicken-Licken in that children's book I read last year? Suppose a felon ambushes the wagon on the way to the carnival and holds us up? Suppose a blizzard hits the county—in which case, this conversation is moot because there wouldn't be no carnival!" She shook her head. "You do too much supposin' and not enough trustin' in the Lord, Guv'ner."

Brent held up his hands in a gesture of surrender, the temples of his glasses dangling from his fingers. "Very well, Miss Evans. If Charleigh and Michael agree, then obviously I'm outvoted. Still, I want you to know that I'm not in favor of taking Joel."

"You've made that clear as windowpane glass. But I think we should give him a chance."

Brent gave an abrupt nod. "I have a test to prepare. I'll see you at dinner."

❧

Days later, while Brent waited for Darcy and Michael to round up the three winners—Joel, Tommy, and Lance—he stared into the cloudless aquamarine sky and wondered again what he'd allowed himself to get into. He watched a formation of birds in their flight south. The scene reminded him of a postcard he'd seen recently detailing a fleet of ships in two neat rows, forming a V. He wondered about Bill and what he was doing. Had his desire to enter the seagoing life given him satisfaction? Or regret? Was he safe from the gangsters' clutches?

A door slammed, and Brent peered over his shoulder. Herbert leaned against the rail of the stoop, Lance next to him. Both redheads had their arms crossed while they talked. The resemblance between the two was striking. They could have been brothers, with their freckled faces and bright eyes full of mischief.

Herbert's expression was envious, but at the same time he seemed grateful. The dressing over his eyes had come off two days ago, and the doctor declared it a miracle that the boy suffered no permanent damage to his sight. He had commended Darcy for her quick thinking in rinsing Herbert's eyes. Darcy had looked uncomfortable at the praise but nodded, saying, "It was Mr. Thomas's idea. All the prayin' every one of us did sure must have helped some too."

Brent thought about the young woman who'd come to the establishment a year ago. In fact, it seemed lately all he did was think about her. A truth that did little to please him. Twice in past months, he'd actually entertained the notion of courting her, then blinked at the absurdity of such an idea and quickly set his mind to the work at hand.

Even now he envisioned her, with her entrancing eyes—as dark blue as the sky sometimes appeared in late autumn after the sun had descended far below the horizon. She'd finally adopted the habit of wearing her dark tresses up, as propriety demanded; but wispy tendrils often trailed at her temples and neck, giving her a delightful air of femininity.

Again the door creaked open. Michael and the last two winners stepped outside. After several seconds elapsed, Darcy followed. Brent blinked, then blinked again, his heart skipping a beat.

Darcy had dressed for the occasion in a cobalt blue dress with a white ruffled inset—obviously an outfit of Charleigh's that had been altered to fit. Yet Brent couldn't imagine it on anyone else. The dress appeared as though it had been designed for Darcy, bringing out the rose of her cheeks and the shine of her hair. The blue hat she wore added to the stunning picture.

She stopped in front of him, offering him a puzzled stare. "Somethin' wrong, Guv'ner?"

Her inquisitive words snapped Brent from his daze. He realized an audience of four watched with amusement and extreme interest. Joel snickered. Brent turned a formidable glance his way and, for good measure, cut it to the other two boys so they would realize from the start that Brent wasn't about to put up with any nonsense. He didn't dare look at Michael.

"Guv'ner?"

Darcy's soft query brought his attention her way. "No, Miss Evans, everything is splendid. Splendid. Allow me to help you to your seat."

Taking her soft, warm hand in his was a mistake, and Brent broke contact the second she was seated on the driver's bench. He felt her curious stare but concentrated on taking his seat and slapping the reins on Polly's back.

Despite Darcy's attempts at conversation, Brent continued to stare ahead, offering abrupt replies to any questions she presented. At last she gave up with a frustrated sigh and turned to watch the thick line of trees on her right while the wagon continued down the road.

Michael and the boys had entered into some sort of rapid word game. Brent shook his head in amusement at the sudden laughter that erupted from the back when Michael missed his cue—probably on purpose in order to gain the lighthearted response he had. He would make a superb grandfather.

Brent had never known his own grandparents. His only sister, Amy, older by eight years, once spoke about them from the little she remembered before they died. Yet they sounded too wonderful to be true; and as a child, Brent asked if Amy were inventing such paragons of benevolence. Whatever the truth, Brent wished he could have known them. Perhaps then he could better understand the concept of fun.

Much later, he pulled the wagon alongside a row of other wagons and several motorcars parked behind makeshift buildings and tents that were part of the carnival. The sun shone pale from a sky that had turned grayish blue, and the distinct smell of roasted peanuts and something sweet made Brent's mouth water.

Unexpectedly, he found himself actually beginning to look forward to the adventure ahead. He decided he would do his utmost to relax and have fun—without sacrificing his dignity or principles, of course. Moreover, he would endeavor not to be stuffy, as the women had dubbed him—first Charleigh, then Darcy.

"Well, my lads," he said, turning to look at the boys with a wide smile. He removed his glasses and placed them in his breast pocket. "Are you prepared to embark on an exciting escapade—one that in all likelihood you shall never forget for the rest of your days on this earth?"

The boys stared. Michael stared. Brent could feel Darcy's stare.

The smile slid from his face. Had he laid the ebullience on a little thick? Perhaps there was a proper way to relax and have fun—one of which he was unaware. Before the day was through, Brent determined to unveil the secret.

# nine

Casting Brent a peculiar look, Darcy grabbed the picnic hamper.

"Leave it be, Lass," Michael said. "We plan to return to the wagon at midday and eat our lunch."

"Of course." She'd already known that, but Brent's bizarre behavior had mystified her and made her act without thinking.

"Besides," Michael continued, "with five strong men to assist, you wouldn't be thinkin' we'd let a wee lass such as yourself carry even a small burden? Isn't that right, laddies?"

The boys responded with a loud chorus of "yessirs."

Darcy grinned. "Michael, you're a peach." She loved the old Irishman. He made her feel like somebody special, like his own daughter.

Brent cleared his throat and stepped down. "Ahem, yes. Shall we proceed?"

Darcy darted a somber glance his way, one he didn't see. Brent would never accept her as a lady, no matter what she did to improve herself. Tommy slipped his hand into hers while the other boys scampered ahead. "Somethin' the matter, Miss Darcy?"

His earnest brown eyes held concern, and she forced a smile. "Nothing for you to fret about. Now, as Mr. Thomas so aptly put it—let's have fun!" She squeezed his plump hand, and he grinned.

At the entrance, a wide banner billowed with the frequent gusts of wind that beat against it and proclaimed in large block letters: RENWALDI'S PREMIER CARNIVAL. Darcy took her first look at the fair. Twin rows of tents and buildings stretched into the distance, sitting closely side by side. The buildings bore elaborately carved and painted fronts. Jewel-colored pennants waved from the top of many. On closer inspection, Darcy saw that the makeshift buildings were narrow in size, and the fronts were false.

A wooden platform extended across the front of every building. One to three carnival workers—easy to recognize because of their outlandish dress—stood on each platform, facing the small crowds that gathered. From what Darcy could see of the aggressive barkers, they enticed anyone with "enough courage" to walk up the five steps and seek the mystery of what lay inside the buildings behind them.

Monstrous mechanical gadgets packed with people whirled round and round. From somewhere within the circular contraption that bore decorated wooden horses, lively organ music played. Laughter, screams, and the sounds of machinery clicking and clanging punctuated the air. Darcy's eyes widened when she noticed a machine built like a huge, spoked wheel. It slowly revolved and took people high—very high—to the top and then *whooshed* them to the ground again to repeat the process. Her stomach lurched just watching the spectacle.

As they moved farther into the noisy, exciting, and somewhat frightening world, the sudden amplified voice of a man captured Darcy's attention. She turned, and the boys followed, as curious as she. They made their way to the platform where a carnival worker stood and bent slightly toward the crowd of onlookers. In one hand he held a bamboo cane, which he waved about with a flourish while he spoke through a megaphone.

"Hurry, hurry—step right up and see Carelli's amazing freak show. The sights inside will astound you. The phenomenon within these four walls will mystify you. See Bruce, the strongest man in the world, lift five hundred pounds. That's right, folks, I said five hundred pounds."

A hairy, well-muscled bald man, wearing no more than a leopard-skin wrap around his thick middle, stepped from beyond the red curtain in the arched center of the false-fronted building. Teeth bared in an awful grimace, he took a stand at the opposite end of the platform. He bent at the waist, held his thick arms bowed out like a gorilla, and growled. A woman onlooker in front shrieked and clapped her hands to her mouth, taking a step back into the growing throng of people. Her companion put his arm around her shoulder in reassurance.

"See Lila, a true freak of nature, and only one of many abnormalities that lie beyond the crimson curtain," the hawker continued. Turning, he gestured with his cane toward the entrance. A young woman stepped from behind the drape to stand on the platform not far from where Darcy stood.

Darcy gasped, the rest of the hawker's speech wafting over her like so much nonsense. Lila's features were feminine, her ringed hands next to her full lilac skirts dainty, her body curved in all the right places. Yet she sported a full curly beard that matched her dark hair. For a moment, her thickly lashed brown eyes met Darcy's sympathetic ones; the bold, indifferent look flickered—but only for a moment. The young woman lifted her whiskered chin and stared Darcy down until she looked away uneasily.

"For only the price of a penny," the hawker continued, "you can witness these shocking freaks of nature and more. But only if you dare." At this, he flashed a wicked smile beneath his waxed handlebar mustache, revealing all his teeth. His last words were a certain lure to ignite every male's determination to prove his courage.

And the boys were no exception.

"Let's go in," Lance cried. "I ain't skeered!"

"I want to see the freaks," Joel said.

"Can we go in, please, Miss Darcy?" Tommy asked, tugging her sleeve.

"I, uh, don't know," she hedged, throwing a glance that cried "help" Brent's way. He looked just as perplexed.

"Perhaps we should find something else to do," he suggested quickly. "It appears that there are many activities to see and do at a carnival."

Obviously he felt as Darcy did. Curiosity had lured them to

listen to the hawker. Shock kept them rooted to the ground through the spiel. But neither wanted to see what lay beyond the crimson curtain.

"Then again, it might do the lads some good," Michael deliberated. "And make them grateful for what they have. I say we take them inside."

Brent and Darcy stared at one another. Michael usually got the last word.

"If you'd rather not go, you can wait here," Brent said, his tone apologetic. "Mr. Larkin and I can oversee the boys in such a confined space."

Darcy gave a slight nod, her gaze traveling to the bearded lady. With a haughty lift of her chin, Lila stared at the crowd ogling her, then turned on her heel and marched back through the curtain. The strong man followed.

"No," Darcy murmured before she could think twice. Something about the bitter woman with the empty eyes caused her to state, "On second thought, I think I'll join you."

⁂

Michael paid their admission, and they took the stairs up to the platform. The hawker held back the heavy velvet curtain as they stepped through the entrance.

Kerosene lamps lit the rectangular room, and swaths of crimson and black material were draped in front of the lanterns, giving off a subdued glow and adding to the mystery. A rough wooden stage with a black curtain that shielded what was beyond took up one entire side of the cramped room, which smelled of newly sawed wood. Wooden folding chairs sat lined up front, and many observers had already taken a seat. Brent motioned to six free chairs in the fourth of five rows.

Once seated, Darcy stared at the curtain. The hawker gave another spiel designed to get every heart pumping with fear of the unknown. Darcy almost changed her mind and left, but at that moment the curtain rose. She gasped, eyes wide. Seated on high stools for the people to gawk at were some of the most pitiful sights she'd ever seen.

Besides the bearded lady and the strong man, there was a man so thin one could see his blue veins, tendons, and bones through his translucent skin. Two young girls joined at the hip were propped against the same stool. A man with a head much too small for his body looked dully out at the audience. A woman so short she would likely come to Darcy's knees stood on one of the stools.

The hawker ordered them to the front, one by one, in order to perform some act that emphasized their deformity. Darcy wrinkled her brow, and fear melted into pity. She watched when a scoffing older boy was given the hawker's permission to pull on the bearded lady's chin to see if her whiskers were real. The woman flinched in pain at the cruel tug. Nervous laughter filtered through the room.

*"I love every one of them, My daughter. And I want you to show them My love, as I have shown My love for you."*

Darcy's eyes opened wide when she heard the gentle voice deep within her spirit—the voice she had come to know this past year through time spent with Him. "How, Lord?"

"Did you say something?" Brent whispered.

Darcy shook her head, not realizing she'd spoken aloud. Again she closed her eyes and concentrated, but she heard no reply to her question.

After the humiliating exhibit ended, the curtain lowered and the crowd was ushered outside. Annoyed, Darcy stood her ground. "May I speak with the others?" she asked the hawker.

"The freaks?" he said in surprise. "Why would you want to speak to them? You a reporter? News reporters are supposed to go through the general manager, Mr. Carson."

"No, I'm not a reporter." Darcy lifted her chin and stared him down, then reminded herself that ladies were supposed to be polite, as Charleigh had taught her. With difficulty, she forced her features into a pleasant expression. "I won't take up much of their time. I only want to talk with them for a few minutes. Perhaps I could just talk to Lila?"

"Sorry, Miss, but fraternizing with the freaks ain't allowed."

He chewed on the stump of a cigar, giving her a level look. "But don't you go botherin' that pretty head o' yours about them. They's fed and well cared for, like all the other animals. So don't you worry none." With that, he strutted back to the entrance, twirling his cane as he did.

Darcy stuck out her tongue at his back. She couldn't help herself. When she realized she probably had an audience of three impressionable boys, she inwardly groaned and turned to face them, wondering how to explain her behavior. Thankfully their attention was engrossed in some dreadful ride on the midway.

Sometimes it was so hard acting respectable, like a Christian was supposed to act. Like a lady was required to act. Sighing noisily, she joined the others. She hoped this particular ride wasn't next on their agenda.

※

As the day progressed, they visited a flea circus, a crazy house of mirrors, and a penny vaudeville featuring a pair of limber dancers. With his flat feet, Brent had never been able to dance well, but he enjoyed watching the spectacle, as he admired all things of beauty.

The boys looked on with bored expressions, obviously not sharing his sentiments. Lance began making rude noises with his hands and armpits, and Michael quickly escorted him outside. Only when a juggler took the stage did the other two boys perk up and strain on the edges of their seats in order to see better.

Throughout the afternoon Brent sent several worried stares Darcy's way. She'd been unusually quiet ever since the freak show. The event had disturbed him as well. Not so much the physical imperfections and abnormalities, though Brent would be lying if he didn't admit to being a bit repulsed. Still, he felt sympathy for those people, who were forced to act like trained monkeys and entertain others.

Remembering the gasps of revulsion and the jeers from the so-called "normal" people in the audience, Brent was reminded

of the games in the ancient Roman colosseum. The only difference he could see between the two was that the Romans
had once held games of sport to kill the flesh. This sideshow
had been designed to kill the spirit of those on exhibit. He
frowned at the memory, wishing to put the event far behind
him. Once the juggler exited the stage, he suggested they eat.

The huge lunch Irma had prepared didn't satisfy the boys,
who insisted on roasted peanuts, candy apples, and other
treats—all of which Michael readily supplied. Brent shook his
head, thinking of the bicarbonate of soda that would likely be
administered to three stomachaches tonight. Four, if Darcy
kept at it. Her disturbance over the sideshow didn't seem to
affect her appetite. Of course, he knew she was partial to fruit,
but three candy apples and a small paper bag of sugared orange
slices was taking it a bit far.

They passed a tall man in a clown suit handing out balloons
to children. The man wore a green-and-white polka-dot shirt
with a yellow bow tie, dark baggy pants, and a tiny hat on his
head. His face was hidden behind layers of white and black
paint, and a huge red frown replaced the usual clown smile.

"Would you like a balloon?" Michael asked the boys.

Joel and Lance both looked the clown's way but shook their
heads. "Naw, them's for babies," Lance said. "Can we ride
that?" He pointed to the upright circular monstrosity with
seats resembling buckets.

"The Ferris wheel," Michael said, nodding. "I don't see
why not."

Joel cocked his head. "You been to a carnival before, Mr.
Larkin? You know the names of all the rides."

Michael smiled. "I've been to Coney Island's amusement
park. It's a lot like this, only on a much grander scale."

As they drew closer to the Ferris wheel, Tommy's face
blanched. "Do we have to ride on that if we don't want to?" he
all but whispered.

Darcy gave his hand a reassuring squeeze. "Of course not.
We can find something else to do while the others ride."

Michael nodded down the midway to the revolving ride with the painted wooden horses attached. "Why not take the lad on the carousel?"

Tommy nodded, smiling. "I do like horses, even if they ain't real."

Joel looked in that direction. "I'd like to go on that too."

Brent stared at him skeptically. He would have figured Joel would be interested in the more thrilling ride.

"I'll take Lance," Michael said. "You two take the others. We'll meet at the hippodrome afterwards."

"And see the Wild West show and the wild animals there?" Lance said hopefully, his eyes wide as he craned his head to look up at Michael.

The old Irishman grinned and ruffled his hair. "Aye. If we're in time for the next show. I t'ink it will be a lot like the circus I was telling you about."

Arrangements made, they went their separate ways.

"Mr. Thomas?"

Brent was only a few yards from the carousel when he heard his name called from behind. He turned to see a patriarch of their small town, one of those in strongest opposition to the reformatory. "Good afternoon, Mr. Forrester," Brent said courteously, though his stomach plummeted in dismay.

"Do my eyes deceive me?" The man's mouth turned down underneath his walruslike white mustache. He adjusted his monocle and gave the boys a scathing glance. "Have you taken these hooligans away from the reform to mix with members of decent society?"

Brent maintained his pleasant smile. "Mr. Forrester, I assure you, all precautions have been taken. These boys are being rewarded for their exemplary behavior—"

"Exemplary!" the old man scorned. "Since when is thievery, lying, and who knows what other fiendish acts cause for reward?"

"It is their changed behavior for which they're being rewarded." Briefly Brent described the contest.

Mr. Forrester's white brows knitted together. "I assume you cleared such a thing with Judge Markham?"

"Everything has been taken into account, Mr. Forrester. Now if you'll excuse me?" Brent tipped his hat, took Joel's hand, and moved away.

"Mark my words, Mr. Thomas, the town council will hear about this," Mr. Forrester called after him. "With criminal activity rampant in your own family, I find it shocking that Mr. Lyons would have left you in charge in the first place. A significant error on his part if this is how you choose to run the institution. . ."

Brent kept walking, though he felt the sharp stab of Mr. Forrester's words. Feelings of anger at Bill flared, and it was with difficulty that he pushed them away.

Darcy took a place beside Brent. "You're doin' a fine job, Guv'ner—the boys are better behaved than I ever did see them. Why, even Charleigh was saying just yesterday how pleased she is with your work at the Refuge."

Brent looked at her. Under the hat, her stormy eyes blazed.

"I cannot take full credit for that," he said. "The boys' improvement is due in part to your ministrations also. It's something we've accomplished together, with a significant amount of help from above."

Darcy stopped walking and stared at him in surprise. A soft smile tilted her lips. "Together. . .we do make a fine team, don't we, Guv'ner?"

Her wistful-sounding words shook him. He couldn't look away from her shining face; and he suddenly longed to stroke her cheek, which appeared as soft as velvet.

A chuckle shook Brent from his trance. He blinked, noticing how people were walking around where he and Darcy stood and stared at each other in the middle of the midway.

"Daydreaming again, Mr. Thomas?" Joel inquired innocently. "Wonder what it's about this time." He snickered and elbowed Tommy in the ribs, earning an answering chuckle from the lad and a stern gaze from Brent.

"Come along," he snapped, his pace faster than before. "We haven't all day to waste at the fairgrounds."

❧

In a daze, Darcy stared at Brent's departing form, then put a hand to the crown of her hat and hurried after him. For one breathless moment, she'd thought he might kiss her—there, in the midst of the crowd, with strains of calliope music coming from somewhere in the midway and mixing with the dreamy music from the carousel. His eyes had been so soft, so full of something that made Darcy's stomach whirl.

"Guv'ner?" she said as she came up behind him and put a hand to his shoulder.

Brent turned, his expression sober. The spark that lit his eyes when he stared at her earlier was gone. "Joel is complaining of a stomachache now and doesn't want to ride," he said, businesslike, his tone holding none of its former warmth. "With all the sweets he ate, I'm not surprised. We shall stand and watch while you take Tommy onto the carousel."

Lips compressed, she nodded curtly and took the boy's hand to lead him away, angry with herself for daring to hope. When would she learn? Brent thought of her—would always think of her—much as one of those poor freaks at the sideshow. It didn't matter how she improved herself; he most certainly would never see the change. She wondered why she bothered, then shook away the thought.

She did it for herself. For Darcy Evans. She wanted to be everything God intended her to be. She enjoyed learning, both in her studies and on being a lady. Her accomplishments made her feel good inside. Darcy lifted her chin with confidence as she stepped onto the stationary wooden disc with Tommy and located two painted horses side by side.

*So much for Brent Thomas,* she thought. She didn't need him or his stuffy ways.

At Tommy's timid request, Darcy took the life-sized horse closest to the outside rim after helping him up on his horse. Perching atop, she drew one leg under her long, full skirt, as though she were riding sidesaddle. With one hand she held onto the metal pole securing the horse to the wooden dais and canopy, while smiling at Tommy and assuring him that the ride wouldn't be a scary one. Pointing to the mirrored column in the middle, she got Tommy to laugh at the silly faces she made at her reflection. Darcy didn't even bother to cast a glance Brent's way, though she knew they were seated on the side where he and Joel stood.

The music of the carousel grew louder as the wheel slowly began to turn and then pick up speed. Darcy clutched her other hand around the pole, holding on for dear life. The cool breeze created by the wheel's movement brushed her face, and any apprehension she had fluttered away.

Suddenly carefree, she plucked off her wide-brimmed hat to let the wind cool her sweat-dampened hair. She laughed, trying to pick out the faces of those who stood watching the carousel spin. But the whole world was off balance, and such a feat proved impossible.

"Grab the ring, Miss Darcy!" Tommy squealed, pointing to a striped pole standing near the carousel. Several gold rings—a little larger than bracelets—hung from a protruding rod at the top. "If you get one, you win a free ride."

"How do you know?" Darcy asked.

"Mr. Larkin told me. Grab the ring!"

Spurred by the boy's excitement, Darcy nodded. With the next revolution, she spotted the candy-striped pole. However, stretching out to retrieve a ring seemed not only impossible but dangerous. Her gaze dropped to the unforgiving hard ground spinning crazily under the edge of the rotating platform. She tightened her grip on the pole. "Aaaee," she cried softly.

"You didn't try for the ring," Tommy said, a pout in his voice.

Darcy took a deep, steadying breath and straightened, waiting for the carousel to take them around again. This time she focused on the top of the pole, refusing to look at the ground. With the brim of her hat securely tucked beneath one knee, she kept her hand solidly fixed around the pole and leaned as far as she could toward the outside, stretching her other hand toward the ring.

"Miss Evans!" Brent's shocked voice came from somewhere within the revolving blur of faces. "What do you think you're doing?"

Her fingers just brushed the metal ring as the carousel took her out of its reach. Now determined, she tightened her grip on the pole and moved farther up on the horse, using her other leg to anchor her to a semikneeling position. The pole came in sight. She slid her hand farther up the slick rail, braced herself, and leaned as far over as she could, her upper body hovering above the ground. Her hat suddenly went sailing into the crowd of onlookers, but her fingers connected with cold metal. She locked her hand around the link and tugged, elated when she came away with the gold ring.

"You did it, Miss Darcy, you did it!" Tommy cried.

A burst of applause from behind almost unseated her. Once she'd settled onto the horse again, she looked over her shoulder. A man with a mustache and dark windblown hair leaned against one of the horses and smiled at her with amused approval in his eyes. Recognizing him as the carousel operator, Darcy hurriedly turned face front.

Her cheeks burned when she remembered the antics she'd gone through for the silly ring. Definitely not in any way ladylike—and what's more, Brent had witnessed the outrageous display. And her hat—her fashionable new blue hat that she'd paid seventy-five cents for! By now it was probably trodden underfoot.

This ride seemed to last longer than the ones she'd watched from afar; and when the carousel finally came to a stop, Darcy was sure the extra time had been deliberate. Especially when the carousel worker sauntered up to her painted horse with a sly smile and extended his hands.

"Need a lift, Miss?"

"No, I'm fine—oh!" Her words shuddered to a stop when she

felt his big hands clasp around her middle and swing her off the horse's painted back to settle her on the wooden planks.

His smile grew more personal. "That gold ring is worth a free ride, you know."

Irritated, Darcy awkwardly sidled past him, the ring clasped to her breast. "Yes, thank you. Another time. Come along, Tommy." She held out her hand to help him down.

"The ride isn't to be missed in the moonlight," the carousel operator called after her. "Come back after dark. There's a full moon out tonight."

Darcy ignored him, heat singeing her cheeks. She still felt a bit dizzy from the ride and clutched Tommy's hand hard as they made their way off the carousel. Tommy looked back at the man, then at her, but he didn't say a word.

Before she could find a familiar face in the crowd of onlookers, Darcy felt her arm clasped from behind.

Brent's eyes were stormy. "And just what was the meaning of that foolhardy exhibition?" He kept hold of her upper arm.

She held up the gold ring. "I won a free ride."

"And you decided to risk life and limb to do so?" he asked incredulously. He shook his head. "Your behavior was appalling; the example you set for the boys atrocious."

Darcy wondered why he was so upset. True, she'd acted a little carelessly, but she'd done a lot worse in the past and never seen him so angry. She forced herself to remain calm. "You're absolutely right, Guv'ner. I did act without thinking. I apologize."

He snorted, something out of place for the proper Brent, and stepped closer. "Who was that man ogling you? What was that all about?"

"Man ogling me?" Darcy uttered in surprise, marveling that he should care. "What man?"

"Don't play coy with me, Miss Evans. I distinctly saw him manhandle you and lift you off that horse."

"Oh, you must mean the carousel operator." She dismissed him with a toss of her hand, though the sudden pounding of her heart belied her indifferent attitude. Could Brent's uncharacteristic behavior actually mean he was jealous? The surprising thought greatly appealed to her womanly ego, and she couldn't help but stoke the fire a bit. "He was just a kindly gentleman helping a lady, is all, and trying to be friendly. Why, he even suggested I take a ride by moonlight," she couldn't resist adding when she saw his eyes narrow. "I have a free one coming, you know."

"Darcy Evans, you steer clear of that carousel worker. He is anything but a kindly gentleman. His kind is after one thing and one thing only. You must guard your reputation and be careful around these carnival workers—in light of your job at the Refuge as a guardian of young boys, of course."

Darcy's eyes widened. Did Brent realize he'd said her first name? Offense quickly replaced wonder when she weighed his words. He must have very little faith in her judgment, telling her whom she wasn't to associate with—as if he had the right! Did he truly think she couldn't see beyond the carousel operator's wily charm and familiar ways? Daily, she had come up against much worse on the streets of East London and knew how to watch out for herself. Suddenly angry, she glared up at him.

"Mr. Thomas, I don't believe I care for your *supercilious* attitude. Now if you'll excuse me, I need to find me hat."

Brent didn't release his hold. Darcy turned, intending to break away, take Tommy, and stalk to the opposite side of the carousel. What did the boys think about their schoolmaster's bizarre display? And he had the audacity to complain about *her* behavior?

Her equilibrium still unsteady, Darcy teetered and suddenly found herself pressed against Brent's chest and in his arms. Staring up at him, she blinked in surprise. He looked down, evidently just as shocked as she.

"Miss Evans, I. . ." His hesitant words trailed off. His gaze magnetized hers and then lowered.

All anger dissolved. She parted her lips in expectation, her pulse rate quickening. His hold tightened, and his piercing blue gaze lifted from her mouth to roam her face. Electric seconds passed, the noise of the crowd vanishing to a muted roar in Darcy's ears. She felt suspended in a fantasy world where everything faded to the background—everything but she and Brent.

"I don't remember what it was that I wanted to say," he whispered, his absorbed expression proof that he was also caught up in whatever held her spellbound.

She lifted her hand to the back of his neck, exerting pressure downward while raising her face to his. Before their lips could touch, he straightened and released his hold on her.

"Miss Evans, you have my most sincere apology," he said, his voice sounding thick. "I don't know what came over me."

Darcy's heart teetered from the clouds and made a fast spiral to the bottom of her chest. Before she could recover, Tommy's high-pitched voice shattered the air, and his hand insistently tugged at her skirt.

"Miss Darcy! Where's Joel?"

# ten

Brent and Darcy stared at one another in shock. Brent was the first to move. "He couldn't have gone far in such a short time."

However, a thorough search of the immediate area did nothing to produce the boy. "You take Tommy and tell Michael what happened. I'll start looking for Joel in that direction." Brent motioned beyond the carousel.

Darcy nodded and hurried toward the hippodrome with Tommy. Brent scanned the crowds in front of each makeshift building and tent. Where could the boy have gone? It had been a mistake to bring him, but of course that was all water under the bridge now. Joel's disappearance was Brent's fault, but he refused to visit that place in his mind. Refused to visit any thoughts that led him to Darcy Evans. He still felt rattled that he'd almost kissed her! Brent shook his head. They must find Joel before he escaped. Where would the boy go? Where would Brent run to if he were Joel?

Brent walked the crowded midway, making a careful scan of each face. Quite a number of boys was scattered throughout the horde, but none of them was Joel. Spotting a muscled, dark-haired man in a pin-striped shirt, he recognized him as the presumptuous carousel worker and frowned. He'd like to give the insolent fellow a piece of his mind.

Brent approached a large tent, eyeing the long row of people waiting to take a turn inside. He doubted Joel would be standing in any line, but it never hurt to be certain.

"Guv'ner!" He heard Darcy's breathless voice from behind him.

Brent quickly faced her. "Have you found him?"

She shook her head. "I only came ter offer me 'elp. Two pairs o' eyes is better than one, I expect. Michael's with Lance and Tommy, lookin' at that end." She pointed to the opposite side of the midway.

Brent would prefer not to be in her company after what happened—or almost happened—between them. Yet she was right: Two pairs of eyes were better than one. And he certainly wouldn't consider letting her go off by herself to search. Not when leeches such as that carousel worker abounded throughout the midway.

Together, Brent and Darcy scouted various attractions, inquiring of different vendors and carnival-goers if they'd seen a towheaded boy, about thirteen years of age, wearing a pair of brown knickers with suspenders and black stockings, a white shirt, and a battered tweed cap. A description that could apply to any number of lads visiting the carnival today, from what Brent could tell.

Twice they were directed to different areas by people who thought they'd seen Joel. Twice they came up empty.

After what must have amounted to half an hour of fruitless searching, Brent realized what had to be done. "I suppose it's time to contact the authorities."

"No," Darcy said. "Let's try a little while longer."

"The longer we wait, the greater a lead he has on us."

Darcy's eyes were troubled. "But if you call the bobbies—I mean, police—you could lose your position at the reform. Who's to say Mr. Forrester won't find out what happened and leak word to Judge Markham? Besides, I don't think Joel ran."

Brent stared at her in disbelief. "How can you say such a thing? It's apparent he did just that. He waited for his chance and took it."

"No." Darcy stubbornly shook her head. "This morning I heard him promise Herbert that he would bring him back a trinket from the carnival. Those two have become close since the fence-paintin' incident. If Joel were plannin' to run, he likely would've confided in Herbert—not led him to believe he would be back."

"Perhaps Joel knew the conversation was being overheard

and only said that to waylay suspicion."

She shook her head again, her lips compressed. "I don't agree. One thing you don't know about criminals, Guv'ner, is that they're a faithful lot—to one another. True, there are some that would betray a friend, but for the most part they's few and far between. Convicts are birds of a feather—an' usually don't keep secrets from one another, 'specially those they come to trust."

Brent considered her words. Darcy should know, having been a former convict. He remembered Bill's revelation concerning family secrets and something else that his brother had said years ago—about felons relying on a code of honor among themselves—as dishonorable and immoral as their actions were. Brent wavered in what steps to take—every second counted—but there was a chance she might be right.

"All right then, Miss Evans, what do you suggest we do?"

She looked at him in frank astonishment. "Why, Guv'ner. I'm surprised you need to ask. We should pray for direction, like we should have done from the beginning. God knows where Joel is, don't He now?"

Darcy took his hand in hers and bowed her head. "Heavenly Father, point us the way to Joel. We ask this in Jesus' name. Amen."

When she looked up, Brent was staring at her in disbelief. A smile flickered on her lips. "Prayers don't need to be long-winded, Guv'ner. Just sincere and from the heart. That's what God looks at," she couldn't resist adding. "The heart. Not what's on a person's outside."

Brent averted his gaze, slipping his hand from hers. "Of course. Shall we proceed?"

For the next several minutes, they searched the south end of the carnival grounds. "Let's try elsewhere." Brent touched her elbow to turn her in another direction, but she stopped and gripped his upper arm.

"Look there, Guv'ner—beyond that sign advertising the fortune-teller. See the small man in the black suit and bowler?

He looks mighty worried 'bout somethin'. He keeps peepin' over his shoulder—though he walks with purpose, as if he knows what he's about. There—see him? He's walking to the back of the tent."

Brent nodded. "It's worth looking into, I suppose."

They followed the short, skinny man around the side. The tents were close together, leaving a narrow walking space, like an alley, that took them to the back. They reached the end, and Brent grasped Darcy's arm when she would have boldly walked onward. Puzzled, she glanced at him.

"We don't know what we're getting into," he whispered. "It's best to proceed with caution."

She nodded, and they carefully looked around the edge of the tent.

Darcy spotted Joel's slim form immediately, and relief almost brought her to her knees. He stood in front of a little table with a man sitting behind it. A shell game was in progress. The man, Darcy noted with surprise, was the clown who had handed out balloons earlier. Some of his face paint was smudged, and his hat and bow tie were gone as well; but the loose polka dot shirt under the yellow suspenders was unmistakable. Both he and Joel were in deep conversation. The man stared intently at the boy, as if he'd found a gold mine. The short man in the bowler had halted his hurried approach and stood, as though uncertain.

Darcy watched while Joel deftly moved three inverted cups round and round on the table, interweaving them with each other. When he stopped, the man said something and pointed to the middle cup. Joel smirked and lifted it to show there was no red ball underneath. A predatory smile lifted the man's painted crimson mouth.

"Eric," the small man said in a surprisingly loud voice. "Carson will have your hide if he knows you're holding illegal shell games with minors. You're on probation now, as it is."

The man behind the table gave a careless wave of one hand, his eyes still on the boy. "Timmons, go back to your flea circus.

Teach the mites to walk a tightrope or something spectacular of that nature." His sardonic voice held a faint European accent. He coughed a few times. "And send more customers my way while you're at it. With this lad's help, I have an idea that will rake in the dough."

The little man shook his head. "You're going to get us both kicked out of the carnival with these ideas of yours." He pointed a shaking finger at the clown. "Find your own customers from now on. I want no part of this any longer. I can't afford to lose this job, even if the pay is peanuts."

The clown looked steadily at Timmons. He rose from his chair in a threatening manner, both palms flat on the table.

Timmons backed down, his smile anxious. "Jewel will help you, Eric. She's sweet on you. And with her informing clients during the fortune-telling that money is soon to come their way from unexpected sources, they're bound to come in droves when she describes you to them."

The clown glared at the man, the frown on his face fiercer than the painted one. "I need no help from a woman!" he spat. "They cannot be trusted. And perhaps neither can you."

Timmons wiped his shining forehead with a kerchief. "I've never failed you, Eric, you know that. But my family needs to eat. Jewel means well. You can trust her."

"You can't trust any woman!" the clown shouted. As if remembering he had an audience, he visibly calmed and looked at the boy. "Timmons, allow me to introduce you to Joel. His talent is remarkable. I'm certain he could teach you a number of tricks as well. Where are you from, Lad?"

"The reformatory for boys in Sothsby. But I'm only there temporary-like, 'til my pop gets out of jail."

"The reformatory. Well, what do you know?" The clown continued to stare at Joel. A slow smile lifted his mouth. "I believe we have some business to discuss." He lowered his voice, making it impossible for Brent and Darcy to hear the rest of the conversation.

"Shouldn't we do something instead of just wastin' our time

standin' here?" Darcy whispered.

Brent shook his head. "The man with whom Joel is consorting has a gun—I saw the strap of a shoulder holster in the opening of his shirt. I think our best course of action would be to wait until Joel removes himself from these unsavory characters and approach him then."

Darcy made a scoffing sound. "Don't be daft, Guv'ner. We can't just stand here an' wait all day."

"Miss Evans, our best plan would be to delay until their conversation is finished—"

"I know his type, and if you aren't going to do anything about it, then I will!" So saying, she jerked her arm free of his light grasp and stepped forward, pasting a curious smile on her face.

"Joel, there you are! I been lookin' for you everywhere."

The two men started in surprise. Joel turned, his expression bordering between guilt and defiance. He stooped to pick up something from the ground, something she hadn't noticed before, and held out what was left of her blue bonnet.

"I found your hat, Miss Darcy," he explained. "I watched some girl pick it up, and I chased her down and made her give it back. I was lookin' to find you when I ran into him." He jerked a thumb toward the clown.

Darcy didn't look the man's way, nor did she ask Joel how he made the girl give him back the hat, deciding she'd rather not know. "Well, that's fine," she said, her tone purposely bright. "But it's time to meet the others now. We don't want to be late for the show. Come along." She held out her hand.

Joel hesitated, looking back at the man behind the table. With alarm, Darcy noticed some sort of understanding pass between them. The clown gave a short nod to the boy, then lifted his gaze to hers. Up close as she was now, Darcy was struck by the evil that radiated from the man's dark blue eyes.

"Come along, Joel," she said firmly. "It's time to go."

Joel grudgingly moved toward her. She grabbed his arm when he came near and walked with him to where Brent waited, concealed at the side of the tent. Brent didn't look at her, didn't say a word, just led them back to the midway. He seemed miffed—with her or Joel, Darcy couldn't tell.

Brent likely held her responsible for what had befallen them, since she had been the one to insist Joel be allowed to attend the carnival. *Some days it just don't pay to get out of bed,* Darcy thought. No matter how hard she tried, it seemed she wound up getting everything wrong.

ﾟ

Days later, Brent stood at the fence and glumly watched a spindly brown colt race toward its mother. His thoughts skittered back to the carnival, and he frowned. Hearing the crunch of footsteps on dry grass, he looked over his shoulder.

"Darcy asked me to fetch you," Michael said as he approached. "She would've come herself, but Herbert is keeping her busy winnowing out the splinter he managed to get into his finger."

Nodding, Brent looked at the horses.

"Somethin' troublin' you, Lad?"

"I'm a failure, Mr. Larkin."

"Sure, and it can't be as bad as all that!" Michael clapped a friendly hand on Brent's shoulder. "You're too hard on yourself."

"No, I *am* a failure," Brent insisted. "At the carnival, I was petrified, afraid that man would pull his gun on us if we revealed ourselves to him. Miss Evans showed more courage than I could ever hope to have. And there have been other times I've proven my cowardice as well."

"And you don't think it takes courage to teach a bunch of lads in trouble with the law? Aye, that it does," Michael said, answering his own question. "There are different types of courage, and you have plenty for the position you're in. When we feel that we're empty, the good Lord gives us what we need."

Brent experienced a sudden strong desire to confide in this man, as he might his father, though his father never had time for Brent's worries or confidences.

"Do you want to know a secret?" Brent lowered his head, ashamed. "Though I was humiliated when they rejected me from fighting in the Great War, I was secretly relieved—and not only because I'd promised Stewart to take charge of the reform. I've inwardly castigated myself for those despicable feelings ever since. What kind of man am I?" He gripped the fence and stared at his white knuckles.

"And do you think the men who fought carried no baggage of fear with them?" Michael asked. "I expect a great many of them did. No one is perfect, Lad. We all have areas of our lives that need work. As you know, many years ago I too showed cowardice—the worst kind—in rejecting me own child."

Brent pondered Michael's sober words. He knew the story of how Charleigh had been born illegitimate, her mother becoming a prostitute in order to care for them. Eight years ago, through an act of God's mercy and grace, Michael was united with his only daughter—who had been under his roof for months, assuming the identity of his niece to escape the man who'd forced her into a life of crime. Brent knew the townspeople still talked of the miracle God had wrought in Michael and Charleigh's lives.

"Aye, Brent, I have a feeling deep in me bones," Michael went on to say, "that when it truly matters and when you desire it most, God will grant you all the courage you need. As He did with the boy David when he faced the mighty Goliath. David knew his source of strength was the Lord—and so will you."

Brent said nothing, only continued to stare at the colt frolicking about the pasture. He hoped Michael was right. Yet at the same time Brent would prefer never having to be in the position to find out.

*Coward.*

He closed his eyes as the word resonated through his mind.

❧

Darcy sat on the edge of Charleigh's bed and related the recurring dream she'd had about Lila, the bearded lady. "I can't explain it, Charleigh. Except to say I know God wants to use me somehow, concerning her. I've had the feeling ever since the day of the carnival. But how?"

Charleigh looked tired but happy, her face flushed. She had only a little over a month until she was due, and the doctor had been very optimistic during his last visit. Not only that, but in spending hours of quiet time with the Lord while resting in her room, she had gained a measure of strength back—both physically and spiritually—and reminded Darcy of the old Charleigh.

"I believe you're right about God wanting to use you to help Lila," Charleigh agreed, leaning back against the propped-up pillows. Her hair was like fire, streaming around her shoulders. "You've been in situations, as I have, that help you to better understand people whom others discard as unworthy. With Stewart and me, God revealed our mission field was this reformatory and helping young criminals to find Him, through showing His love. I'm convinced God has a wondrous plan for your life as well and will reveal it to you as He sees fit."

Darcy nodded, encouraged by Charleigh's words. "By the way, I noticed a motorcar leave as Michael and I returned from town. Did someone come to visit?"

Charleigh's brows gathered into a frown. "Judge Markham came by to discuss the carnival outing with Brent. It seems Mr. Forrester complained, feeling it his duty. That man has been a thorn in our side for years and has tried to close us down every chance he gets."

"What did the judge say?" Darcy asked.

Charleigh shrugged. "Brent didn't tell me, but he didn't seem too upset. So I gather everything went well."

Darcy grew thoughtful. "I wonder if Brent told the judge of Joel's disappearance and how we found him. Likely not, since the boy was playing a shell game at the time."

Charleigh looked surprised. "A shell game?"

"Didn't I tell you? I thought I had. We found Joel behind a

tent with a man dressed as a clown. The man was in deep conversation with Joel—apparently either givin' advice or receivin' it, concernin' the game." Darcy shivered, remembering the man's wicked eyes. "Definitely not someone we would want Joel to associate with."

"I should think not! Shell games are illegal." Charleigh grew sober, contemplative. "What did the man look like? We should report him to the authorities, especially if he's consorting with children."

"I think it's too late for that," Darcy mused, wondering why she hadn't thought of it before. "I heard in town today that the carnival pulls out tonight."

"Hmm. Perhaps. Still, it wouldn't hurt to report him."

Darcy thought a moment, then straightened. Charleigh's words suddenly made the clearest sense. "You're right!" She rose from the bed, knowing what the Lord would have her do. "Can you manage for a few hours without me or Brent at the reform?"

Charleigh looked curious, but nodded. "The boys are doing their chores. Father and Alice are here, so everything should be fine."

"Then I'll see you this evening."

"But where are you going?"

Darcy smiled. "I'll tell you about it later—if I'm successful. Right now, I have some convincin' to do on someone else." With a wide smile, she winked and hurried out the door. Before going downstairs, she went to her room and retrieved the purchase she'd made in town last week. At the time she didn't understand what led her to buy the book, since she had one similar. Now she did.

She found Brent in the parlor. "Good!" Darcy exclaimed. "Now I don't have to go in search of you."

He raised his brows. "You wish to speak with me?"

"Aye. That I do. Might as well grab your hat, Guv'ner. We have somewhere to go." Darcy whisked toward the door and plucked her shawl from a wall peg.

"Somewhere to go?" Brent's confused voice echoed from behind.

Darcy lifted her battered blue bonnet from the hat tree and pulled the hatpin from the crown.

"Miss Evans, will you kindly inform me what this latest flurry of activity is all about?"

Darcy slapped the bonnet over her head, deciding to dispense with the pin this time, since her hair was braided to her waist. There hadn't been time to put it up this morning.

"*Miss Evans.*" His tone was impatient.

She turned. "It's quite simple, really. You're taking me to the carnival. We'd better get a move on, since they'll be leavin' soon."

His mouth dropped open. "I'm taking you to the. . ." He shook his head as though to clear it. "And do tell what has put such a preposterous notion into your head?"

She shrugged. "If you don't take me, then I'll go by meself—or ask Michael to drive me, though I'd rather not, since he took me to town once today. Oh, and Charleigh did give her approval. But not to worry, Guv'ner. If you can't spare the time, I'm not afraid to go alone." Tapping her crown, she gave him a quirky smile and strolled outside.

Muttering under his breath, Brent grabbed his hat and hurried out the door after her.

# eleven

For the first mile of the ride, Brent remained quiet. Darcy didn't mind; she had enough to think about. Like how she would approach Lila and what she would say once she did. Darcy only hoped that the irritating barker wasn't around to thwart her plans. *Thwart.* Her new word for the day.

Darcy peered at her companion. Sitting rigid as ever, Brent held the reins in a strong grip, his jaw as tight as his fists. She shook her head.

"No need to look so dour, Guv'ner. It's not like I kidnapped you or forced your hand in takin' me. I told you I was willin' to go alone. Anyway, Charleigh did say they can do without us for a few hours, and the day is quite lovely." She inhaled deeply, lifting her face to the cloudy sky and putting her hand to the crown of her hat. "Just smell that crisp air! It's a wonder you can actually smell cold weather, isn't it?"

Brent gave a curt nod, and Darcy looked away, resigned to enjoy the day alone.

"Perhaps you wouldn't mind telling me just why it is that we're embarking on this little outing," Brent said wryly after a few moments elapsed.

"Why, Guv'ner—all you had to do was ask." At his startled glance, she threw him a saucy grin. "I need to talk to someone at the carnival, though I've no idea what I'll say. It's just something I feel the Lord's impressin' me to do."

Brent was silent, as though assimilating her words.

"And while I'm about me business, you should report the shell game incident."

"Pardon?"

"The clown who was with Joel—and from the looks of it, trying to get him to join his illegal activities. He should be reported, don't you think? So that he doesn't pollute another child's mind with his nefarious ways."

Brent stared at her, evidently surprised. He didn't remark on her fancy new word—by now she'd collected a hefty bundle of them—but rather arched his brow as if in thought.

"You're absolutely right, Miss Evans. I was so caught up in transporting the boys safely back to the reformatory that I didn't speculate on the matter. The man definitely should be reported, and I intend to do just that. How astute of you to think of it."

Darcy pulled off her hat and fiddled with the ribbon above the brim. "I can't take full credit. Charleigh is the one who suggested it." What was she doing? For once, Brent was offering her a sincere compliment not related to her education, and she was flinging it back in his face? Still, she didn't want praise if it wasn't rightly deserved.

He gave her an odd look, one that Darcy couldn't decipher, but he didn't reply.

Soon they arrived at the carnival grounds. In the soft gray light of overcast skies, Darcy saw the midway had taken on a dramatic transformation. Gone were the hordes of people, the barkers, the calliope music. The false fronts had been taken down, and the tents and makeshift buildings were being dismantled by workers too busy to notice Darcy and Brent's presence. The cool breeze picked up numerous leaflets, paper sacks, and other bits of discarded trash, sending them skidding over the ground as though they had a life of their own.

Darcy peered in the direction of the freak show. Her heart sank to see the building gone. Where would she find Lila?

Almost in answer to her mental question, the woman came walking around the corner of a tent and crossed the midway. In her arms she held a beautiful dark-haired child, possibly two years old. As she walked, Lila bounced the girl, who laughed with glee.

"Do 'gain!" the tot cried, clapping her hands. "Do 'gain!"

Lila caught sight of Darcy and halted in surprise. Wariness

flitted through her eyes before she stiffly resumed walking, ignoring Brent and Darcy.

"Excuse me," Darcy said when the woman was only feet away. "I'd like to talk with you." She moved closer so she could be heard over the racket the workers made. "Me name's Darcy Evans."

Lila directed somber brown eyes at Darcy. "The freak show is over. Go home." She started to walk away.

Unfazed by the woman's abrupt words, Darcy hurried forward. "It isn't the show I've come to see you about."

"No?" The woman stopped and tilted her head in evident dis-interest. "If you're a reporter, I'm not available for questioning, and I'm not interested in an interview." She clutched the child tighter to her breast. "I have nothing to say to the public."

"I'm not a reporter." When Lila remained unapproachable, Darcy deliberated, wondering how to convince her. She dropped her gaze to the wide-eyed child, who hooked one chubby arm around Lila's neck and stared at Darcy with uncertainty. "That's a gorgeous little girl you have there. Is she yours?"

Lila cocked a wry brow. "Surprised a freak can give birth to a normal child?"

"I didn't say that." Darcy gave an exasperated sigh. The woman was obviously bent on being difficult. "Can we go somewhere to talk? I mean no harm, and I won't take up much of your time."

Lila hesitated a long moment, eyeing Darcy, then gave a curt nod. "This way, then."

Darcy glanced at Brent before following Lila to a set of railroad tracks nearby, where the carnival train sat. On the side of each railcar were words painted in red, yellow, and blue, labeling the different attractions. Lila stepped up to one of the trailer cars and cast a brief glance back at Darcy before continuing into the car, which contained sleeping berths. She moved down the narrow aisle to one of the lower berths and gently deposited the child on a thin, dirty mattress.

"There now, Angel." Lila brushed the curly black locks from the girl's forehead and bent to kiss her pink cheek. "Time for all good girls to take a nap."

The girl pouted. "Don' want sweep. Want Mama an' Unka Buce."

"Mama has to take care of things so we can go bye-bye on the train tonight. And Uncle Bruce has to help the men take things down. But beautiful, bright-eyed girls named Angel must go to dreamland now." She tickled the girl's side, making her giggle, then grabbed a faded doll from the mattress and placed it in the girl's arms. "Sleep well, precious Angel. Mama will be back soon."

Lila stood, pulled the curtain that covered the berth closed, then looked at Darcy, her eyes cold again. "We can talk outside."

They exited the sleeping car, and immediately Lila faced Darcy, crossing her arms in a defensive gesture. "Just what do you want from me?"

Instead of answering, Darcy asked a question of her own. "Where is the child's father? Is he with the carnival too?"

"Why do you want to know?"

"Just curious—it's a fault of mine. You don't have to tell me if you don't want to."

Lila paused, considering. Though her expression was indifferent, pain glimmered in her eyes. "I haven't the faintest idea where Angel's father is," she said at last. "Nor who he is. Late one night when we were at a small town in Jersey, I needed to make a quick trip into the nearby woods and was attacked in the dark. Angel was born nine months later. And though I'll always despise that lecher for what he did to me, I wouldn't trade anything for the joy that sweet child has brought these past two years."

Darcy nodded, unsure how to reply.

Lila's cold gaze traveled over Darcy's altered dress. "I suppose my story shocks you, since you come from a good home and have no concept of what pain or hardship means."

Darcy straightened to her full height and worked to keep her voice level. "A good home? Hardly. After me mum died, when I was ten, me stepfather came after me. I whacked him over the head with a frying pan and ran away. I lived on the streets of London and begged for me food. When the beggin' brought no pence, I stole what I could to feed me belly; and later, when I was older, I relied nightly on the numbing effect of ale. No, Lila, I didn't know any good thing except for the friendship of three other guttersnipes—who are now either dead or in jail and were as miserable as I."

Lila's cold disinterest melted as Darcy spoke. "Then you know how hard life can be."

"Aye, that I do. But I know somethin' else. Somethin' I never knew 'til someone told me. And though I'm not well educated in how to speak me mind, I came to share with you the truth I found. The truth a friend taught me. God loves you, Lila. He wants you to know it."

Lila stared in disbelief and gave a scoffing laugh. "You expect me to believe that? I suppose God loved me so much He decided to tack a beard and mustache to my face for good measure—making it impossible for any man to love me. Is that what you're saying?"

"All I know, Lila, is that God is not cruel and vindictive; He's lovin' and full of peace. He died on a cross so that ye could be with Him forever. All He asks is that ye accept His sacrifice and follow Him. He truly does love you. He sent me here to tell ye so."

"Did He now?" The words were mocking and harsh, but vulnerability flickered in Lila's brown eyes. "And just what else did He tell you?"

"He asked me to give you this." Darcy pulled the small book from the bag she carried.

Lila stared at it.

"It's a Bible."

"I know what it is," Lila snapped. Her gaze—cold again—

lifted to Darcy's. "I know all about sacrifices too. My father was a preacher. Surprised? I sensed how uncomfortable he was around me—how he couldn't stand to even look at me, and I overheard him tell my aunt one night of the sacrifice he'd made to raise me, of the burden God had given him. Knowing I wasn't wanted, I sneaked away from home four years ago when this carnival came to town, and I joined up with it."

Darcy didn't know what else to say or why the Lord had even directed her to come. Lila was hardened to hearing anything about the gospel. And she knew what was in the Good Book, if her father was a preacher. "Well, that's all I had to say, so I'll be leavin' now. I did so want to help you, but I can't force you to receive the message of God's love. Good-bye, Lila. I'll pray for ye tonight—and every night from here on out. You have me word on that." She tucked the Bible into Lila's crossed arms and moved away.

"Wait!"

Darcy turned in surprise.

Lila seemed uncertain. "Did you mean what you said? That you want to help?" Biting her lip, she uncrossed one arm, took the Bible in her hand, and moved a step toward Darcy. "This carnival is no place for Angel. I want her to live a normal life—or as normal as can be with a mother who's a freak. Do you think. . .can I come work for you? I'm a hard worker and am skilled in housekeeping, sewing, and cooking. I make all my own clothes and Angel's too. My mother died when I was twelve, and I had to take over those duties while I lived with my father."

Seeing Darcy's eyes widen, she hastened to add, "I promise I'll stay out of your way and won't come anywhere near when your friends are around. I can shave off this beard, so I'd appear normal. The reason I haven't is a fear I've had since childhood—when I accidentally cut myself deep enough to produce a scar—and the idea of using a straight razor every day on my face is frightening. My hands aren't always steady, but I'll do it if I must. No one need know of my deformity. If

I could bear to give up Angel, I'd ask you to take only her. But without her in my life, I'd surely die."

Darcy searched for something to say. "Lila, I can't hire you."

The woman's features hardened. "Never mind. It was foolish to ask. I suppose you're like those who have no problem speaking the gospel, but when it comes to living it, that's another matter altogether. I shouldn't be surprised. You might as well take this back. I've had enough of your kind to last me an eternity." Lila stuffed the Bible into Darcy's hand and moved away.

"Now you wait just one minute," Darcy snapped. "It has nothing to do with any such foolishness. I live at a boys' reformatory—a place for young criminals. The boys there can be cruel—believe me, I know—and bringing you home with me would be like bringing a lamb to wolves."

Lila shook her head, unconcerned. "I've heard every insult there is and am accustomed to being gawked at. I could handle any taunts and jeers. I'm only concerned about my Angel. Would she be unsafe there?"

"I've been there over a year, and while the boys are in definite need of reformin', they would never hurt anyone. Of that I'm sure." Darcy blinked, realizing what she'd done. Instead of dissuading Lila, she'd given her reason to further plead her cause.

"I have no authority to hire you on, Lila. Neither does Brent Thomas, the schoolmaster there and the man I drove here with. All decisions are made by a small board of members at the reform. Brent is only one member of that board."

"The carnival doesn't leave until late tonight," Lila said quickly. "If your people disagree to the arrangement, I'll return here. I promise. And if that should happen, we'll find our own transport back so you won't be bothered with taking us."

Darcy hesitated. "What about Angel's uncle? Won't he miss her?"

"Angel's uncle? Oh, you must mean Bruce. He's the strong man in the freak show—no relation. Angel dotes on him and he on her. It would be hard for both Angel and me to leave him—he's been a good friend—but as I said before, I only want what's best for my daughter. And I don't like some of the things that's been going on at this carnival lately." She quickly broke off as though she'd said too much. "Please, Miss Evans?"

Darcy studied the entreating, desperate eyes. She thought of Charleigh, of her kind and generous heart and tarnished past. She thought of Michael, who never condemned a soul and was always ready to help someone in need. She thought of Stewart, whose main objective in opening the reformatory was to help those nobody wanted. The hopeless cases. The outcasts.

Sighing, Darcy nodded. "Grab your daughter, and come along, then."

She didn't dare think of what Brent would say.

❦

"What in the name of all that is sane and normal were you thinking, Miss Evans?" Brent stared at Darcy, exasperation written on his face. "Have you lost all the good sense God gave you?"

They stood in a sheltered part of the woods near a creek. Lila was in the wagon changing Angel's diaper. This was their first moment alone since Darcy had returned to Brent with Lila and Angel in tow.

"I know Charleigh," Darcy insisted. "She would've done the same."

"Would she now?" Brent shook his head and started to pace again, threading his fingers through his hair—an uncustomary action for him. He'd left his hat in the wagon, and for a moment Darcy admired the way the sunlight through the trees picked out threads of bronze-gold in his tousled locks. "Yes, perhaps she might have, as it *is* her place to acquire any help needed at the reformatory. But *you* had no right to do so! There is already an efficient cook and housekeeper at Lyons's Refuge, and you were hired as the cook's assistant. What will that woman do at the institution?"

"That woman?" Darcy crossed her arms. "Tell me, Guv'ner,

this isn't about Lila's qualifications at all, is it? It's about her appearance."

Brent tensed and faced her. "What do you mean?"

"What do I mean?" Darcy scoffed. "Why, surely you could tell she sports a beard, couldn't you, Guv'ner? But of course you could! Outside appearances are of great importance to you, aren't they now? Unfortunately, you can't see past them to the heart that beats inside. More's the pity."

A muscle twitched near his jaw as he approached. "Miss Evans, this conversation is highly irregular as well as being entirely preposterous—"

"Is it now?" she interrupted. "Preposterous, ye say? Then tell me why it is that ye've not noticed the changes I've made in the past year? Tell me why when you look at me you still see an uncouth, brash girl spoutin' Cockney. Well, all right, I may still be brash and slip into Cockney at times, but except for that poetry contest, ye've barely given me credit for any changes made! And I've tried—oh, how I've tried to win yer approval. I studied hard—harder than you know, harder than any o' the boys. I stayed up late night after night to learn how to be a better person—a lady you would admire, maybe even tyke a fancy to. But did it do any good, I ask you? No! Not that I care to impress you any longer. You're too busy judgin' on outward appearances and retainin' early impressions to give a person any room to change or see what lies on the inside— where God looks, I'll remind you again. And I pity you your ignorance and stony heart."

Darcy began to pace, then looked back and retraced her steps toward him, her annoyance not yet sated. "And with someone like Lila—who likely can never alter her appearance—you can't see beyond that to her heart, which is so pure and good and fine that the only thing she wants out of life is to do the best she can for her little girl. Well, Mr. Stuffed-Shirt Thomas, more's the pity for you!" She leaned forward and snapped her fingers beneath his nose. "And that's what I think o' that!"

Brent stood a moment, unblinking. Suddenly he grasped her upper arms, his eyes flaming. Her own eyes went wide in shock at his unexpected reaction.

"You think I don't care about people—that I don't have feelings? Oh, I have feelings, I assure you. I may not understand you, Darcy Evans, but I've definitely noticed you. I may not always commend you for your progress, but I've seen you excel in numerous areas and have been proud of your accomplishments. Keep in mind that I'm flesh and blood—not a 'stuffed shirt,' as you call it. Why, a few times this past week I almost kissed you—" Brent broke off, his face darkening in embarrassment. Hastily he lowered his hands to his sides. "Forgive me. That was uncalled for."

Before he could move away, Darcy spoke. "Well, why didn't you?"

He hesitated. "Why didn't I what?"

"Kiss me."

He looked uncomfortable. "Miss Evans, I strongly recommend that we cease this conversation."

"The name's Darcy, Guv'ner. I've heard you use it before." She tilted her head. "I want to know what stopped you from kissing me—like ye said ye almost did."

Brent released an exasperated sigh. "We were in a public place. Such a display hardly would have been appropriate."

"This place seems private enough."

He blinked, his mouth dropping open as the meaning of her soft words hit him. "Miss Evans. . ." His voice cracked.

"Try again. It's Darcy."

"Darcy." He said the name tentatively. "Perhaps we should continue this conversation another time. I believe we should return to the wagon. Your friend will wonder what's happened to us." He turned to walk away.

Darcy acted, instinctively knowing that if she didn't do something, he never would. Hurrying up behind him, she put her hand to his shoulder and tugged. "Brent, wait."

He turned to face her, surprise on his features. Before she

lost courage, she plucked off his spectacles, wrapped her arms around his neck, and planted a solid kiss on his mouth.

Warm tingles coursed through her, but he stood as stiff as one of the tree trunks surrounding them. Darcy was about to pull back in humiliated disappointment when suddenly his arms wrapped around her, pulling her close. His lips began to move over hers, sending her into a dreamlike trance from which she never wanted to emerge. After several seconds elapsed, Brent lifted his head and gazed at her, a heart-melting mixture of desire and surprise glimmering in his blue eyes.

Keeping her arms around his neck and grateful he hadn't removed his hands from the middle of her back, Darcy studied his face. "What now, Guv'ner?" she asked quietly. "Where do we go from here?"

He shook his head. "I don't rightly know." His voice was hoarse.

"Well, then, may I make a suggestion until we arrive at a decision?" Putting her hand to the back of his head, she brought his face down to hers and kissed him again.

This time his response was nothing like that of a tree trunk.

# twelve

Hungry for something to tide him over until dinner, Brent rotated the knob of the back door leading to the kitchen. He stopped in surprise to see Lila sitting on a wooden chair, her back rigid, her eyes squeezed shut. A towel was draped under her chin. Alice stood next to her, gently sliding a straight razor over one cheek covered with white foam.

"Don't move, Lila," Alice gently warned. "There's nothing to be afraid of—nothing to this, really. I often give Michael a shave. And he's told me plenty a time I shoulda been a surgeon, what with my steady hands and all." She gave a self-conscious, almost girlish, giggle.

Uneasy at the sight of a woman being shaved, Brent closed the door with a quiet click and stepped off the porch. Two days had passed since Lila arrived at Lyons's Refuge. Darcy had been right. Charleigh and Michael welcomed her and her daughter with open arms, though some of the boys had been less than chivalrous. Lila stared at them while they spouted their malicious jibes and laughed sardonically after each one. Once the last verbal weapon was slung, she merely lifted an eyebrow and asked, "Are you finished yet? Because if that's all you can think of, let me tell you I've heard it all before. And, quite frankly, I'm bored with the sameness. Now, if you'll excuse me." With that she'd taken Angel in her arms and marched upstairs to her room—to the unease of six dazed boys, who'd been given extra work duties that evening for their cruelty.

Brent stared at the thick bank of murky clouds in the distance. The wind had picked up in the last hour, a herald of the coming storm. Brent hoped Michael would return to the Refuge before the weather broke. He'd driven the wagon to his home, Larkin's Glen, to check on things there.

Brent watched the long, wheat-colored grasses bend underneath the weight of the chilling wind, as though bowing in submission to a force greater than they. Several bare branches of a nearby oak clattered against the fence at regular intervals when a sudden strong gust shook them. Brent's thoughts skittered to the accusation Darcy had hurled at him in the woods during their drive home from the carnival. Was she right? Was he judgmental, seeing people's appearances only and not their character within?

Since Lila had come to the Refuge, Brent invented excuses to stay away from her, uncomfortable with her presence, even a trifle disgusted when looking at her—though she'd worn a dark blue veil as a harem girl might, to hide the beard. He didn't admire his feelings, knew they were anything but charitable, but he couldn't seem to help them. He'd been appalled by Bill, not only with his choice of lifestyle but also with his preference for flamboyant clothing. He'd found fault with Darcy when she first came to the Refuge—her Cockney, her clothing, her manner. . . .

Brent closed his eyes. Not only was he a coward, he *was* hypercritical of others.

"Heavenly Father," he muttered, "I don't desire to feel this way. I don't want to be judgmental and always finding fault. Help me, Lord, to love as You would love, no matter the outside appearances. Help me to see through to the heart as Darcy does, as Charleigh does—even as Michael does. To see true heart appearances and not merely the outward shell—"

"Guv'ner?"

Brent tensed at the suddenness of Darcy's voice behind him. The loud whisper of wind in the grasses had masked the sound of her approach. Had she heard his soft prayer? Slowly, he turned to face her.

Her hair hung in one braid to her waist, as she often wore it. Several long, dark tendrils had worked themselves loose around her face.

Unsettled with how close she stood, Brent took a hasty step backward, the recent memory of their kiss in the woods rushing to the forefront of his mind. He had enjoyed the feel of her in his arms that day—indeed, had allowed the kiss to linger, even forgetting about Lila waiting in the wagon. Yet once he'd broken the embrace, the impropriety of the situation assaulted him; and he was thunderstruck by his unseemly behavior.

Cocking her head, Darcy looked at him with those smoky blue eyes. "Are you feeling all right? You look a mite pale."

"I'm well."

She frowned. "You don't look it." She pushed up one sleeve and lifted her forearm to his forehead, propelling him to take another step backward—a half step really, since his back came up against the wooden fence. "If you do have a fever, it's not high, though your face looks rather flushed now."

"I told you I'm fine," Brent snapped.

Her chin lifted. "Well, maybe your health is fine, but your disposition could sure use some improvin', and that's a fact! Ever since the day we brought Lila home, you've been snappin' like a turtle and avoidin' me like a turkey does a fox."

Brent chose not to answer. He took a deep breath and reached for his handkerchief to clean his glasses. The cloth wasn't there. He'd forgotten to tuck one into his pocket that morning. In fact, since their initial trip to the carnival, he found himself doing a lot of things out of character for him.

Feeling somewhat cornered, Brent took a sideways step, sliding along the fence and hoping he wasn't causing his new suit coat irreparable damage. He wanted to place himself in a more comfortable position with plenty of room between them. Nervously he cleared his throat. "About that day, Miss Evans—"

"So we're back to formal names, are we?"

"I owe you an apology," he continued as though she hadn't spoken. "My untoward behavior was totally uncalled-for, and I regret that you were a recipient."

❧

"Untoward behavior?"

His face darkened another shade. "The incident in the woods."

She scrunched her brows together. "Now let me get this straight. You're apologizin' for kissin' me?"

"Yes. My actions were reprehensible."

Darcy determined to look up that word the first chance she got. She had a feeling it wasn't good. "You're making much of nothin', Guv'ner. It was just a kiss."

"Be that as it may, in polite society such behavior isn't considered acceptable. If two people do choose to go courting, holding hands should be the limit of physical contact they share—weeks after the courtship commences, of course." Brent pulled at his collar as if it were too tight. "Although a chaste kiss on the cheek when parting is allowed, I do believe—"

"Sounds dull as salt what's lost its flavorin'."

He looked at her, stunned. "Pardon?"

"Who made such stuffy rules? You? And what does courtin' mean anyway?"

His mouth compressed into an offended line. "Courting is how things are done in a genteel society, Miss Evans."

"But there's no feeling to anything like that! It's like a rule book to follow instead of affection to share." She crossed her arms. "Oh, get that scandalized look out of your eye, Guv'ner. I'm not suggesting anything improper. People aren't machines that ye wind a crank and out comes the same response. People have feelings, and they shouldn't have to bottle them up until a specific time states they're allowed to exhibit them."

Slowly uncrossing her arms, she stepped closer. "Why, if I wanted to put my hand to your cheek like this," she murmured, lightly cradling his jaw, "why shouldn't I be allowed to? I'm not hurtin' no one. And I'm showin' you what's in me heart."

"Rules are important," he stated, his voice coming out

hoarse. "Guidelines are needed."

Darcy frowned, dropping her hand away. "Ye make it sound as if I'm suggestin' something illicit. I'm not, I told you. And I've given a black eye to those who've tried—and that's a fact!"

ॐ

Brent didn't doubt it for a minute. He also didn't doubt that it was past time to end this conversation.

"Perhaps Mrs. Lyons could better instruct you on the topic of courting and all that it entails if you wish to know more. I have papers to grade. Good day, Miss Evans." He gave her a slight tip of his hat and hurried to the schoolhouse before she could say another word.

ॐ

"That man is so irritating, Lord," Darcy grumbled as she stood at her window later that night, watching light sleet fall from a dark sky. "It's a wonder I feel the way I do about him. Just for a moment, there in the woods, I thought he'd unbent his stiff ways—just for a moment, mind You. Yet he hasn't changed one bit, has he? He's the same as always. Straitlaced, solemn, and oh, so noble—"

Darcy's words broke off as realization struck her a swift blow. Was she doing the same thing she'd accused Brent of? Judging merely on outward appearances and not seeing through to the heart of the man inside?

Her eyes fluttered closed. She was doing exactly that! And had been for quite awhile. How many times had she labeled Brent proper, stuffy? She may have put on a good show of accepting others at face value, but in her heart she'd been as guilty as Brent. And just as judgmental.

"Oh, Jesus, I'm ever so sorry. Make me more tolerant of others, no matter what their shortcomings. Make me more sympathetic of things—and people—I don't understand."

All of a sudden Darcy caught the image of what looked like a slight form hunched over and running toward the barn. She pressed closer to the window. Positioning both hands around her eyes to block the light from the room's electric torch, she squinted through the blurred pane to try and see any kind of movement outside. She rubbed moisture away from the glass and watched as the dim form worked the barn door open.

So she hadn't been imagining things! From inside the barn, a lantern issued a feeble glow. The boy's cap fell off, revealing a thatch of hair, shining ivory in the pale light. He reclaimed his cap and entered the barn, shutting the door behind himself.

Joel! What mischief was he up to now—and in this kind of weather to boot?

Darcy rushed downstairs, grabbed her cloak, and threw it about her shoulders. Glancing at the parlor door, she considered telling Charleigh where she was going but dismissed the idea. Charleigh had overtaxed herself today, making a rare appearance downstairs to read to the boys, with the excuse that she was sick and tired of the four walls of her room. After the story, Alice had insisted Charleigh rest on the sofa, where she'd fallen asleep minutes later.

Darcy hurried through the front door, the pelting sleet harsher to her ears now that she stood in the midst of it. Before heading toward the barn, she glanced at the schoolhouse. Hazy light glowed in the window near Brent's desk. *He must be grading papers again.* Darcy considered acquiring his aid or at least informing him of the situation. Yet Brent was still angry with Joel for running off at the carnival—no matter that the boy said he'd only done so to rescue her hat. Darcy wasn't certain why Joel was skulking about; but if the boy had a plausible excuse for being in the barn when he should be in bed, Brent might be annoyed with her for bothering him. Or he might be unnecessarily harsh with Joel. Brent had been so unlike himself lately, and Darcy decided she would rather take care of this matter on her own.

With her decision made, she pulled the cloak's hood over her head and carefully made her way through the slippery grass toward the barn. The sleet fell heavier than before; and by the time she was halfway there, her thick stockings inside her shoes felt damp with icy water. Her irritation with Joel increased. He'd better have an awfully good reason for being in the barn this time of night!

At the old building, Darcy struggled to open the heavy wooden door enough to slip inside. She peered around the dimly lit barn and up to the loft on the other side, near where the horses and cows were penned in their stalls.

"Joel?" Her voice wavered in the chill air, which smelled of manure and wet hay. "I know you're here. I saw you from my window."

A horse's soft whinny and snort was the only reply.

Swallowing her irritation, Darcy stepped toward the lantern light flickering on the crude board walls.

"Joel, talk to me," she said, her eyes trained on the pale yellow light. "You know you're not supposed to be outside the house after dark. Is something upsetting you? Maybe I can help." She stopped suddenly. The light. She had seen the lantern before Joel entered the barn. Which meant—

"Joel, who's here with you? Herbert? Lance?" When eerie silence met her demands, she frowned. "Very well, Joel. If you—and whoever else is here—don't come out this minute and tell me what this is about, then you leave me no alternative but to enlist the aid of the substitute headmaster. And you'll receive a much harsher discipline than ye normally would have for breaking curfew, of that I can assure you."

Before she could say more, a man's arm clapped across her chest, followed by the ominous click of metal near her ear— the sound of a gun's trigger being cocked.

Darcy struggled for balance as her shoulder blades pressed against the man's heaving chest. The cold steel barrel of the pistol bit into her scalp, and fear swallowed her whole.

"I hardly think that will be necessary," the man rasped close to her ear. "*Now* you play by my rules."

❧

Brent set down his pen and rotated his shoulders, trying to work out the kinks from sitting in one position too long. His mind traveled to Darcy, as it frequently had since he started grading today's tests. In fact, it would be wise to go over the marks he'd made a second time, since his mind hadn't been entirely on his job.

He sighed and looked out the sleet-spattered window. This afternoon's conversation with her had been uncomfortable, to say the least; still, he was unable to cease thinking of it.

Did he wish to court her? They were so dissimilar to one another, yet there was something about being in her presence that made him feel whole. As though she contained an element missing in his nature. Brave, loyal, fun-loving—Darcy was all those things and more. Yet, what did he have to offer in return?

He was a reject. A failure. How could he promise protection in the possible role of her husband when courage for him was as unreachable as the moon? Michael's words floated to his memory. "When it truly matters and when you need it most, God will give you the courage you need."

Brent removed his spectacles and closed his eyes. He wished he could be certain. He had faith in God; that wasn't the problem. Rather, he entertained little faith in his own ability to carry through if the situation should warrant it.

Sighing, he folded the temples of his spectacles, opened his desk drawer, and laid them inside. He purposely had not attended dinner at the main house that evening, wanting to avoid Darcy, but he was hungry now. Knowing Darcy, she likely had put something aside for him.

After grabbing his overcoat and hat, Brent turned down the kerosene lamp and moved toward the door.

❧

"Be still!"

Darcy recognized the faintly accented voice of the man holding the gun to her head. It was the clown from the carnival.

"What do you want with me?" she asked, maintaining a show of bravado though her heart beat with the fury of a panicked bird. "Why are you here?"

He chuckled, then coughed. Darcy could feel his body

tremble and noticed how heat seemed to radiate from him. He was obviously quite ill.

"You cost me my job," he growled through his teeth. "Word spread of how one of the freaks left with a lady Brit to work at a boys' reformatory." He coughed, the sound raspier. "When I was fired after a stranger informed my boss of my 'illegal activities'—only minutes after you and your boyfriend left with Lila—it wasn't hard to figure out. Especially after making your acquaintance behind the fortune-teller's tent last week." A severe bout of coughing shook him.

Darcy swallowed. "You're ill. You need care."

"The only thing I need now is vengeance!" he growled in a low voice, pressing the barrel harder to her head. "This day was long in coming. I've waited for it for years, and neither you nor anyone else is going to rob me of my satisfaction."

Darcy furrowed her brow. "Long in coming? What do you mean? You're not making sense." The fever must be giving him delusions.

"Shut up!" he ordered. "We three are going to the main house now, and you're going to lead the way. But I warn you. One false move, and I'll blow you to kingdom come. I'm an expert marksman."

Darcy turned to face her attacker. She'd been right in her assumption regarding his identity. In the lamp's glow, she could see his aristocratic features were sickly pale, almost gaunt, with shadows under his eyes. He wore no overcoat, only a pair of trousers with a shirt and suspenders and a shoulder holster under one arm. He was thin, his body shivering. Sweat-dampened hair clung to his head. In his hand he held a gun—now trained at her heart.

"We haven't any money if that's what you're after." Immediately Darcy thought about her remaining three and a half dollars and flinched, but he seemed not to notice.

"That's not what I'm after," he said. "It's a simple matter of justice. And revenge."

Darcy said nothing, wondering how someone of his caliber

could equate the word *justice* with his dark motives.

"Mister, you said no one was going to get hurt." Joel's uncertain voice came from somewhere behind Darcy. "I told you I'd go with you. Just leave her and the others alone."

Rage ignited in the man's eyes as they snapped toward the boy. "Joel, as my new associate, you must learn never to talk back to your superior." His low words were smooth but full of undisguised venom. "I'll not have it."

"Yes, Sir," the boy whispered, his voice barely audible above the sound of sleet falling on the roof.

The man returned his gaze to Darcy, a smile lifting the corners of his cracked lips. "Actually, Joel, you're about to learn an important lesson in the art of seeking justice from those who've wronged you. Keep your eyes and ears open. There may be a test afterwards." He chuckled, then coughed and motioned with his gun toward the door. "After you, Miss. And, remember, if you want your friends to remain alive, I'd advise you not to do anything foolish."

Keeping her expression blank, Darcy moved in the direction he indicated, trying not to let him see her fear.

# thirteen

Brent let himself in through the kitchen door and lit a nearby lamp, preferring its soft glow to the harsh glare of the electric light. He felt like a boy sneaking into the kitchen after hours for a late-night snack. He opened the icebox and crouched to peer inside. Hmmm. Interesting. The bowl there appeared to contain a vegetable mix with strips of chicken. He wondered if Darcy had made it. She was a wonderful cook.

The unmistakable sound of the front door flying open, then slamming shut, broke the silence. Brent shot to a standing position and faced the hallway entrance. Who would be up this time of the night? Darcy? Samuel? Or had Michael returned?

About to call out, he changed his mind. The household was surely asleep; and if the sound of the front door hadn't awakened anyone, Brent certainly didn't want to. Nine boys were difficult to get back to bed.

Curious, he shut the icebox and crept along the hallway. He heard a man's low voice—not Michael's or Samuel's—in the parlor. Suddenly Charleigh gave a soft cry of fright.

"Eric!" she exclaimed as though she'd seen a ghost.

Alarmed, but instinctively knowing he must remain silent, Brent peered around the corner. In the light of a lantern Joel held, Darcy sat wide-eyed next to a pale Charleigh on the sofa. All three were staring at a tall man who pointed a gun at the two women. Brent's mouth went dry.

The man chuckled. "*Bonsoir*, dear Charleigh. Destiny brings us together yet again. I've waited for this day a long time, and the Fates were kind enough to drop the opportunity into my lap."

Shaking her head in shocked denial, Charleigh pulled the

blanket closer around her shoulders. "But—but Stewart told me years ago that he'd read an account of your death in the paper!"

"Yet, as you can see, I'm not dead," Eric said with a slight wave of his gun.

"A dockworker identified your body!" Charleigh insisted, as though by saying it, she could make it true.

"Men will do anything for money. And his price wasn't so steep." Eric coughed. "I found the need to, shall we say, disappear. Some of my former associates in Manhattan were out to kill me."

"Imagine that," Charleigh muttered sarcastically. "So you murdered another poor soul to lose your identity?"

Eric shrugged. "Actually, no. Someone had already done the deed. I stumbled across his corpse one night on the docks, saw my chance, and took it. The dockworker fixed his face so no one would recognize him."

During the conversation, Darcy repeatedly looked in confusion from Eric to Charleigh. She spoke for the first time. "You know this man?"

"Yes," Charleigh said bitterly. "This is the man who was with me on the *Titanic*. The man I assisted for three years in a life of crime. Darcy Evans, meet Eric Fontaneau—the cruelest man alive."

"Fontaine, now," Eric said, his manner almost glib. "After disposing of my alias, Philip Rawlins, with the dead man, I took back my real name—only changed the surname to sound more American. And I tried to lose the French accent, though a trace has quite obviously remained." Again he coughed.

Brent grasped the edge of the wall, remembering the despicable things Stewart had told him about this man. And he was here now with Darcy and Charleigh, his intentions boding evil. Brent couldn't simply stand by and allow these women to remain in danger. He couldn't! Yet what could he do? The man was armed. Brent knew Stewart kept several guns locked in his study, but he didn't know where the key to the glass case was—and even if he did, he didn't know how to fire a weapon. The phone was too close to use. Even if he whispered, he would be overheard.

"What do you intend to do with us?" Charleigh asked. "Why are you here?"

"Why am I here?" Eric repeated, almost cordially. He moved, and Brent zipped back around the corner to avoid detection, waited a moment, then looked again. Eric was now seated in the rocking chair facing the sofa, his gun still trained on the women.

"Well, dear Charleigh, since you ask, originally I planned to take both you and Joel from this place and resume our 'life of crime'—isn't that how you put it?" He chuckled, then coughed again, harsher this time. When the spell ended, he waved the gun toward Charleigh. His gaze lowered to her rounded belly. "Yet, in your present condition, my plan to use you as bait will no longer work."

"I did my time, Eric," Charleigh seethed. "I went to a reformatory and paid for my crimes. And I will not return to that life again!" She straightened, lifting her chin. "I want you out of my house—now."

"I hardly think you're in a position to make demands," Eric said. He leaned toward her, his jaw rigid. "I told you once before that I don't like my women to talk back. You would do well to remember that."

Darcy put a protective arm across Charleigh's chest. "She's not your woman. She never was."

"Indeed?" Eric sounded amused. "I beg to differ, Miss Evans. She has always belonged to me."

"Stewart paid you—" Charleigh began.

Eric waved his gun to silence her. "Did you honestly think I would agree to his stipulations? You're mine, Charleigh. I'll admit, when you foolishly turned yourself over to Scotland Yard and were sentenced to the reformatory, that little setback altered my plans for us. And your present condition certainly isn't going to help matters. Regardless, you're coming with me."

"No!"

To Brent's horror, Darcy rocketed up from the couch, her hands flying to her hips, her face flushed with anger. She seemed suddenly oblivious to the gun Eric turned her way.

"Sit down," he ordered impatiently.

"Ye won't harm a hair on her head, ye won't," Darcy bit out. Instead of sitting down, she took another step forward, making Brent's heart lurch in fear. "I heard about what you done to her—how you made her think she was married to you all those years when she wasn't, how you beat her and ended up killin' the baby she carried—"

"Darcy, no!" Charleigh whispered.

Eric swung his shocked gaze toward Charleigh. "Baby? You were carrying my child and didn't tell me?"

Charleigh's expression grew bitter. "It doesn't matter any longer. I'm another man's wife, and I carry his child. I'm also a Christian and have repented of the former life I led."

"How touching," Eric said in disdain.

Brent surveyed the room, knowing he must do something soon. Suddenly Joel turned his head and met his gaze. Brent tensed. The boy studied him for a few eternal seconds. "Mr. Fontaine?" Joel asked, gaining the man's attention.

Brent frantically considered what to do if the boy should reveal his presence. Should he run up and surprise Eric before Joel could speak? And do. . .what? He ran a hand through his damp hair. How could he stop Eric?

"What is it, Joel?" Eric asked impatiently.

"We can make it fine—just us. I'm a fast learner, and I'll show you everything my pop taught me, if you want to know. We don't need no skirt along. My pop once said that women-folk just get in the way of a man's business. . . ."

Brent listened in amazement, realizing what Joel was doing. He was diverting Eric's attention so that Brent could act. Again, Brent's gaze swept the room—and landed on Michael's pipe, which sat on its stand on a nearby piecrust table. An idea struck. A rather lame idea, but it was an idea.

*God, help me.*

Moving from behind the wall, Brent crept toward the stand, the carpet underneath his feet muffling his footsteps. He grabbed the pipe and slowly made his way toward Eric.

❧

Darcy watched, baffled, as Brent crept up behind Eric holding a pipe. A pipe? Had he gone daft? What was he doing? Was he going to suggest they smoke a peace pipe and have a pow-wow like her history book said the Indians once did?

Brent caught her eye and shook his head. Immediately Darcy looked away.

"In most cases, I would agree with you, Joel," Eric replied. "Women cannot be trusted. Yet when someone takes what's yours—as Mr. Lyons did to me—justice must be met. He won't have her again; of that I'll make certain."

"You're not going to kill her, are you?" the boy asked fearfully, eyes wide.

"No," Eric said, "but I'll kill anyone who stands in my way this time." He cocked the hammer of his gun and stared at Darcy. "Anyone."

From the corner of her eye, Darcy saw Brent falter. She swallowed hard, silently begging God to shield his presence. He advanced the last few feet to Eric's chair. Lifting his arm, he pushed the stem of the pipe against Eric's upper back. The man gave a startled jump.

"No," Brent said, his voice surprisingly calm. "I don't imagine you'll harm anyone, Mr. Fontaine. Now be so good as to drop the gun."

Eric moved to turn, but Brent jabbed the pipe stem harder against his shirt. "*Now*, if you please."

Eric complied, and Brent looked at the boy. "Joel, please retrieve the weapon and bring it to me."

Joel looked uncertainly between the two men for an excruciating moment, then nodded and picked up the gun from the carpet, handing it to Brent. Brent pocketed the pipe and held the gun.

"Now, put your hands in the air and slowly turn around," Brent said.

Eric did so, his eyes widening. "Bill? What are you doing here?"

Brent looked confused for a moment, then said, "If the man to whom you're referring is Bill Thomas, he's my brother."

Eric looked taken aback. "Except for your clothing, you could be twins."

"So I've been told." Brent glanced at Darcy. "Please, Miss Evans, retrieve some rope to tie up our guest."

Eric's gaze grew calculating. "Actually, I remember Bill talking quite a bit about you. Brent is your name. He mentioned you were the timid sort. Afraid of your own shadow, he said. Certainly not the type to use a gun on anyone."

Darcy wrinkled her brow. This wasn't going well.

"Get the rope," Brent ordered again, his voice wavering.

Before Darcy could move to comply, Eric lunged at Brent, and both men fell to the ground. Darcy stared in horror as Eric pulled back his fist and hit Brent in the jaw twice, then reached for the gun. Brent held his own, throwing a few surprisingly well-placed punches. Eric's weakness worked against him, and soon Brent had the upper hand as both men fought for possession of the gun.

A deafening shot cracked the air.

Both men fell slack.

Darcy screamed.

# fourteen

Surprise covered Eric's face as he put a hand to his side. A spot of crimson quickly spread across his shirt. "I've been shot."

Brent stared at the gun in his hand. He looked at the two women, his eyes disbelieving. "I didn't mean to shoot. The gun went off without me realizing it—"

"Mercy! What's going on in this place now?" Irma cried as she rounded the corner in her nightcap and robe. She gasped when she saw Eric lying prone on the floor.

"Irma, ring for the police," Darcy said, taking charge. "And get some hot water and bandages."

Irma hustled off, and Darcy stared down at Eric, tilting her head and crossing her arms. "Though we should just dump you outside in the sleet or maybe put you in the barn with the other animals, my Christian training won't allow that." She turned to Charleigh, who still looked pale. "Where should we put him?"

"Here," Charleigh said, rising from the sofa and protectively clutching her middle.

Irma hustled back in. "The phone's not working. I'll get the bandages and water."

With Darcy's help, Brent lifted Eric onto the couch. The wounded man moaned, closing his eyes. Alice and Lila soon joined them, demanding to know what the ruckus was about. Several boys plodded downstairs in their nightshirts and bare feet.

"What's going on?" Lance asked, curiously peering around the corner into the parlor.

"Nothing that concerns you." Lila moved to block their vision and shooed them away. "Back to bed, all of you."

Darcy turned to the spot where she'd last seen Brent, but he was gone.

❧

Brent stroked his throbbing jaw and stared out the kitchen window at the sleet, which had turned to snow a few minutes ago. Though the hour was late, the household was awake. All were too nervous to retire to their quarters with a murderer under their roof, even if the man was seriously injured. Brent's thoughts went to Bill, and he shook his head. Obviously Eric knew his brother well.

"Brent?" Darcy's low voice came from behind him.

He tensed but didn't look at her. She touched his sleeve and came around to stand in front of him. "Thank you for saving our lives," she said. "You're a hero."

Brent shook his head. "I almost killed a man."

"Before he had a chance to kill us," she shot back softly. Her fingertips stroked his cheek, and he flinched. "Does it hurt?"

"No," he lied, enjoying her touch too much.

She smiled. "Aren't you the one who's taught me and the boys to always speak the truth?"

"You're right," he amended. "I apologize."

"I can chip off some ice from the block in the icebox. That should take the swelling down."

Swelling? That would explain why the lower part of his face felt as if it were on fire.

"You look like a squirrel hoarding nuts in its cheeks," she added. "Your lip is bleeding too."

Brent felt for his handkerchief. Realizing he didn't have it, he gingerly wiped the corner of his mouth with his knuckles.

Darcy fetched a dishcloth and wet it with water from the pump. "Joel confessed that at the carnival Eric promised he would help the boy find his father if Joel would join up with him. But when Joel heard Eric and Charleigh talk tonight, he decided Eric was bad news." She returned to Brent and dabbed gently at his lip with the wet cloth. "He could've gone with Eric and left us all to whatever fate Eric had planned. Perhaps this is the heart change we've been looking for in Joel."

"Perhaps." Brent was mesmerized by her liquid dark eyes, as

deep and mysterious as an indigo sky.

"Charleigh won't sleep. She's edgy and upset. She won't confide in me, and I don't know what to say to her. But it can't be a good thing for the baby, her staying up all night and pacing the floor like she's doing." Her gaze lifted to his. "Alice said Eric was only nicked, though with all the blood he lost I'm amazed. She mentioned his illness might be what's made his blood thinner—though of course she's no doctor. Still, I think she stitched him up well."

"I have faith in her abilities," Brent said quietly.

Darcy pulled the cloth from his mouth but didn't move away. "Irma said the roads are probably icy. We might not get help for some time."

"I'll stay in the main house until help arrives."

"That would be nice."

He fidgeted, nervous, yet unable to look away from her. "I'm relieved that you survived the ordeal."

She smiled. "I feel the same about you."

He cleared his throat. "Well, I must check on our prisoner."

Releasing a frustrated breath, Darcy grasped his coat lapels before he could leave. "Can't you forget about etiquette for once? I almost lost you in there—you could have been killed. I could have been killed! If it's wrong for me to break society's courtin' rules and express me feelings, then so be it, but express me feelin's I will!"

She wrapped her arms around his neck in a hug and kissed him gently. At first Brent tensed, not so much from shock but from pain. Even her soft lips caused him agony. She pulled away with a sad sigh.

"You know, Guv'ner, you could easily discourage a girl. If I didn't suspect you liked me too, I'd give up. I just might at that. One too many rejections, and a girl soon gets the message." Shaking her head in disappointment, she gave him one last look before leaving the kitchen.

Brent made an effort to gather his wits about him. He would analyze her words another time. Right now, there was something he must know.

Determined, he headed for the parlor and stared at the wounded man on the sofa. A lantern burned on the table beside Eric. He opened his eyes and stared up at Brent, his expression wary.

Brent came straight to the point. "How do you know my brother?"

Eric paused a long moment. "He was with a gang I joined up with in Manhattan," he said at last. "He warned me that my life was in danger and put his own life on the line to do it. He was like that, always trying to prevent someone from getting hurt."

Brent stared, taken aback. Bill had saved this man? Is that what had put Bill's life in jeopardy? Perhaps Brent had judged his brother too harshly. He didn't understand what made Bill do the things he did, but Brent was relieved to hear that his brother wasn't as black as he'd painted him, even if the life he saved was that of a criminal's.

"Thank you for telling me." Brent moved away.

"Bill was wrong about you," Eric said, his raspy voice filled with grudging respect. "You're no coward. In fact, you're alike in many ways."

Brent smiled, though it made his jaw ache. Any credit for courage he owed to God.

❧

The phone lines were still down the following day, with more snow falling. Darcy looked toward Eric, who lay on the sofa and stared up at the ceiling, his expression sullen. He'd barely spoken a word all afternoon, though he'd eaten the stew Irma brought him.

Darcy stretched in the rocker and set down her book. It was agreed that every adult take a watch over the prisoner, and Darcy's vigil was almost over. Any moment now Brent would walk in for the night shift. Since Darcy's kiss in the kitchen last night, he'd become more distant; and Darcy resolutely made up her mind that she would leave him be from now on.

If he wanted a relationship, he would have to be the one to make the first move.

Footsteps sounded in the hall. Expecting to see Brent, Darcy was surprised when Charleigh rounded the corner.

"Charleigh? Shouldn't you be in bed?" she asked.

"There's something I must do," Charleigh said, determined. She glanced toward Eric. At her entrance he had peered her way, then quickly looked back to the ceiling. Charleigh waddled toward him, her hands clenched into fists at her sides.

"Eric, I have something to say to you." When he didn't respond, she stepped closer. "Look at me!"

At her demanding words, his gaze narrowed on her.

"You made my life miserable and taught me the meaning of true fear. And though I've every reason to despise you for all you've done—" She took a deep breath. "I choose to forgive you. I know it's what God wants, because He's been dealing with me ever since you got here. He forgave all my sins, and I can do no less when it comes to you."

His expression remained unchanged, but he didn't look away.

"I don't expect you to understand." She hesitated. "Anyway, that's all I have to say." She turned to go.

"Charleigh, wait," he whispered, wincing and clutching his side. "You've gained courage since we were together. How did this come about?"

"If I have courage, it's because of God. I know He'll stand up for me, so I'm not afraid to speak. Nor am I afraid of you anymore."

He studied her in silence, then turned his sober gaze to the ceiling again. Charleigh left the room.

When Brent came to relieve Darcy, she gave him a polite smile—no more—and went to her room to lie down. Yet she couldn't rest. Charleigh's act of forgiveness stirred something deep within her, bringing to the surface something she knew the Lord was telling her to do.

"Oh, Lord, no. Please. Not him." She sat at her bureau, her

gaze lifted to the mirror. In her dark, beseeching eyes, she recognized the truth.

❧

The next morning the phone was working, and Irma called the police. Michael arrived at the same time they did. "What's going on?" he asked as he walked through the door behind one of the officers. "Did one of the boys get into trouble? The weather kept me stranded at home or I would have come sooner."

Alice grabbed his arm with an affectionate squeeze, pulling him past the parlor entrance. "Everything's fine now. I'll tell you all about it over a cup of coffee. I'm just so glad to have you with me again." She moved with him in the direction of the kitchen. Obviously she was concerned about Michael's reaction when he learned of Eric's presence, considering what the Frenchman had once done to Charleigh.

Frowning, Brent watched as Darcy swept past without looking at him. She'd been avoiding him since yesterday. Clutching something tightly in her hand, she walked toward the sofa. Two policemen helped Eric to stand, one on each side of him. Though he was still weak and shaky, handcuffs circled his wrists in front. Darcy stopped close to Eric.

When she said nothing, he raised a mocking eyebrow. "Well?"

"Right," she said and stuffed a few crumpled bills into his hand. "For you to buy an overcoat. You're in desperate need of one."

The bills fluttered to the carpet. Darcy picked them up and tucked them back between his fingers.

"You're giving me money to buy a coat?" he asked incredulously.

"That's right. Three dollars. It should be enough. If there's any left over, you can buy a pair of gloves too."

"Why? Why are you doing this?"

"Because you need a coat. You're ill. And, well, I felt the Lord tell me to give you the money."

Disbelief filled Eric's eyes as he stared down at the three crumpled bills. "I could have robbed you," he said quietly. "I held a gun to your head and might have killed you. And you're giving me money to buy a coat?"

Darcy smiled brightly. "Life sure is strange, isn't it? But then Christians are often called a peculiar people." She sobered. "I once promised God I would do all I could for the needy, having come from just such a situation. I even wrote a poem about it—that's where the money came from. I won it because of me poem. And last night the Lord reminded me of my vow and told me to give you the money."

Several seconds of quiet elapsed.

"No one's ever given me anything," Eric murmured as he stared at the bills in his clasped hands. Moisture glistened in his eyes when he looked up. "Not even my father, except for the nightly beatings when he'd had too much wine. My mother left him when I was too small to remember. I had to fight, tooth and nail, for everything I had. . . ." He looked away, embarrassed for disclosing a part of his past. Glancing at Darcy once more, he offered a swift nod. The policemen on either side grabbed his upper arms and escorted him to the door.

"I shall pray for you, Eric," Charleigh said before they stepped outside. "That you find the Truth that will set you free."

He halted, the policemen also stopping, and looked her way. There was no malice in his eyes, only bewilderment. "Why? Why would you pray for me after all I've done to you?"

"Because I've learned that true forgiveness means not only forgetting the past. It also means refusing to punish the person who's wronged you, while holding their best interests at heart."

Eric shook his head. "I don't understand."

Charleigh smiled. "Perhaps not now. But I feel strongly in my heart that one day you will. God go with you, Eric."

Brent stood in the entrance and watched while the two policemen slowly escorted the shaky man to their motorcar. Darcy came to stand beside him.

"That was a noble gesture, giving him that money," he said, relieved she was no longer avoiding him.

Darcy offered a faint smile, then moved away without a word. Frustrated, Brent watched her go.

❧

Darcy stood in the loft and used a pitchfork to toss hay below. Months had passed since the night Eric disrupted their lives, at the same time bringing all of them into a closer understanding of true Christianity. Spring had come and with it a sense of release for Darcy.

Throughout the long winter, Brent remained distant, though often Darcy would catch him watching her. Yet she kept her vow not to push herself on him. She still cared for Brent; in fact, her feelings had deepened despite the distance between them. Still, Darcy had learned something. It wasn't all that important if Brent accepted her or if anyone else did, for that matter. As Alice often told her, she couldn't please everyone. God loved her for who she was, and she liked herself. That was all that truly mattered.

She straightened to wipe perspiration from her brow and then bent to shovel another forkful of hay and toss it onto the growing mound. She needed to hurry. She had promised to help with Charleigh's new baby, Clementine, while Alice and Irma went to town and Charleigh got some much-needed rest. Clementine had been born the day after Christmas, healthy and beautiful, bringing joy to all their lives.

"Miss Evans!"

Startled to hear Brent's voice directly below, Darcy peered over the loft. He stared up at her, his hair and suit sprinkled with the hay she'd just tossed.

"Oh, sorry, Guv'ner!" she apologized, giggling.

"If you're sorry, why are you laughing?"

She grinned. "It's just that you look so funny!"

"Hmmm. Be that as it may, I have something I wish to discuss with you."

His sober tone sent warning bells ringing inside Darcy. "Not now. I'm finishing up Tommy's job—since he's been sick with those awful stomach cramps." She turned to shovel up another forkful.

"If that's for the animals, you could feed the town's livestock on what you have down here."

Wrinkling her brow, she stared at the towering mound. Had she pitched too much hay? She wasn't familiar with the chore.

"Very well," Brent said. "I'll come up there."

Darcy blinked. "You'll come up here?" she said, watching as he climbed the ladder. He reached the top rung and she backed up, made uneasy by the determined look in his bright blue eyes. She noticed he wasn't wearing his spectacles.

"Really, Guv'ner, I'll be down in a jiffy. There's no need for you to come up."

"Too late," he said as he stepped onto the loft's wooden floor.

She clutched the handle of the pitchfork, uncertain. His strange, intense behavior rattled her. Before she could think about what she was doing, Darcy tossed the pitchfork aside and jumped onto the high mound below. She landed with a loud rustle, the lumpy hay prickling her through her dress.

"Wait, don't go!" Brent called. To her surprise, another rustle filled her ears as he landed on the mound beside her. He grabbed her arm before she could scramble away. "Why did you jump?" he asked.

"Because you're actin' so peculiar!"

He shook his head in exasperation, giving her a wry grin. "You know, Darcy Evans, you make it extremely difficult for a man to make the first move."

Her mouth dropped open. "Guv'ner?"

"Brent," he corrected, drawing her close. "The name is Brent." And with that, he kissed her like he'd never kissed her before.

When he pulled away, Darcy stared, dazed and breathless. "Did you really kiss me?" she whispered, still not believing it.

"Yes, I did. And I intend to do so every day we have left together on this earth. That is, if you'll have me."

"You're askin' me to marry you?"

"I am. Frankly, I don't know how I existed this long without you." His gaze softened. "You taught me to enjoy life and to look beyond outward appearances—to the heart. And, Darcy, your heart is so selfless and pure and beautiful, always wanting to do good—a man would have to be a fool not to love you."

She smiled, hardly daring to believe what she was hearing. "You love me?"

"I denied it for a long time, but, yes, I love you dearly."

"Oh—and I love you dearly too!" She hugged him hard, but her joy flickered as a thought came to her. "Does this mean we'll be courting the full year?" Alice had informed Darcy about courting, also telling her that many considered it outdated.

Disappointment glimmered in Brent's eyes. "If you would prefer to, we can. Yet, due to our long association, I don't feel a short engagement would be inappropriate."

"Good! But keep in mind, I'll likely always be brash and speak me mind. Often the Cockney slips out despite my best efforts to speak right."

"And I shall likely oftentimes be stuffy." A pained look crossed his face.

Darcy laughed. She couldn't help herself. She loved this man so much—especially covered with hay as he was now. He looked anything but stuffy!

He plucked a piece of straw from her hair. "Something amuses you, Miss Evans?"

"Nothing, Guv'ner," she said, her smile wide. "Nothing ter squawk habout anyways."

Brent laughed at the familiar phrase.

"And the answer is yes—I'll marry you as soon as you like. In fact, the sooner the better, as far as I'm concerned! Does tomorrow sound all right with you?"

He shook his head, his eyes dancing. "Oh, Darcy. However did I survive my bleak life until you came along?"

Before she could think of a response, he pulled her close and kissed her again.

# epilogue

Darcy stood beside her husband of seven weeks and stared at the magnificent sunset. "I'm going to miss Lila and Angel," she murmured. Brent slipped a comforting arm around her waist, and she settled her head on his shoulder. Her fingertips brushed the edge of her jacket. A gift from Lila.

Yesterday, while trying to decide what to pack, Lila had thrown her colorful garments into a heap on the floor, stating she wanted no reminders of her carnival days and intended to burn them. Darcy had been horrified to see the gorgeous red jacket with Chinese embroidery and gold buttons cast onto the pile. Seeing Darcy longingly eye the crimson satin, Lila lifted it from the heap and placed it around her shoulders, rendering Darcy speechless. Not only was the jacket a perfect fit, it was ten times prettier than the jacket the organ grinder's monkey wore all those years ago, when she was a child.

Joy over the long-desired treasure mixed with sadness upon losing a friend. Lila and Angel were leaving the Refuge tomorrow. It had been a shock when Bruce, the strong man from the carnival, showed up at the door last week, begging to see Lila. Concerned, Darcy eavesdropped and heard Bruce vow his love, telling Lila she was the sole reason he'd stayed with the carnival. Judging from the shy smile Lila offered when she later informed Charleigh and Darcy of her impending marriage, Darcy knew Bruce's feelings were returned; and she was happy for her friend. One thing was certain: Lila and Angel would always be in her prayers.

"I'm amazed at how well Joel has taken to Lila," Brent said thoughtfully. "Especially since he was her worst tormentor those first few weeks she was here."

"It is amazing, isn't it?" Darcy asked. To everyone's shock, the two had grown close. After his experience with Eric, Joel changed. He still talked incessantly of finding his father one day, but he wasn't as volatile as before. He'd grown considerate of others, conscientious in his studies, and rarely started a fight with any of the boys.

"Well, I best be seeing to the baby," Charleigh said from her post by the porch rail. She moved to go, then stopped. "Oh dear, isn't that Mr. Forrester's car? What does he want now?"

Darcy peered up the lane toward the gate. Sure enough, a black motorcar with a bent fender chugged their way.

"He's probably found something else to bicker about." Charleigh blew out a frustrated breath. "Honestly! It seems that man has nothing better to do than meddle in our affairs and try to find a reason for closing us down."

A sudden wail reached them from inside.

"Clemmie," Darcy said to Charleigh. "Go. I'll take care of Mr. Forrester."

With a grateful nod, Charleigh hurried inside.

"Darcy," Brent warned.

She flashed him a smile. "In a nice way, of course."

"Perhaps you'd better let me handle this," Brent suggested as the car rolled to a stop. "Especially after the way you lit into that peddler last week for his derogatory comments about Lila when he spotted Alice shaving her—" His words broke off as he stared at the vehicle.

Looking thinner and tired, Stewart patted the side of the car and motioned a farewell to the driver. A scrawny young boy in ill-fitting clothes stood off to the side. Mr. Forrester offered a feeble smile and drove away while Stewart hurried up the steps. He clasped Brent's hand in a heartfelt shake and accepted Darcy's welcoming hug.

"Delighted to have you back," Brent said.

"You could have told Charleigh your plans," Darcy lightly admonished. "I do believe she was beginning to wonder if you were ever coming home."

"Darcy," Brent said.

"No, she's right," Stewart replied, his voice hoarse. "Things have been rough. Mother almost lost her home, and I had to intervene. Then I got sick, and there were other problems too."

"Stewart." Charleigh's disbelieving whisper reached them.

His gaze whipped past Darcy's shoulder, and he moved the few yards toward his wife, though he didn't take her in his arms as Darcy thought he might. He looked awkward, standing there, and Darcy's heart went out to him.

"Forgive me, Charleigh. Forgive me for staying away." His voice came low. Brent averted his gaze, but Darcy watched the reunion out of concern for her friend. Charleigh nodded but looked as uneasy as Stewart did.

"I need to tell you something. Something that might help you understand why I had to go." Stewart hesitated. "Since the war's end, I've dealt with some tough issues. You were depressed about losing the babies, and I didn't feel I should burden you, but now you need to know. Two days before the fighting ended, a good friend of mine, a lieutenant, died in my arms in the trenches because he obeyed my orders."

"Oh, Stewart." Charleigh clasped her hands in her skirt, seeming at a loss.

"I won a medal for saving others, but I couldn't save Rudy," he continued, as though he had to get the words out quickly before he lost courage to say them. "I failed him. A good man depended on me and died. Eventually I convinced myself that you'd be better off without me too—that I'd brought you nothing but heartache—"

"No, that's not true."

"Please, Charleigh, let me finish. I'm telling you this now because in mending the breach with my family and helping them, I began to heal. But it wasn't until I was laid up with the flu and had idle time that I saw how unfair I was being to you, by not sharing what I was going through. And by staying away. I was wrong. I decided that as soon as I recovered, I'd come home and somehow make it up to you. So here I am." He lifted his hands upward. "That is, if I'm still welcome."

"Of course you're welcome," Charleigh whispered. "But you're not the only one at fault, Stewart. I was wrong too. I was so absorbed in self-pity, thinking only of myself at the time, that I wasn't even aware you were hurting and needed me."

Unmoving, they stared at one another, then closed the short distance between them until they were in each other's arms, murmuring words of love and forgiveness. "I'll never stay away again, Charleigh," Stewart said. "You're all the world to me."

Tears stung Darcy's eyes, and Brent drew her close. "Perhaps we should go inside," he whispered. Darcy nodded, and they moved to go.

Stewart pulled away from his wife, keeping her within the circle of his arms. "Please, wait—both of you. There's someone I want you to meet." He looked toward the child still standing where the car had left him off. "Clint, come here."

The scruffy-looking boy hesitated, then, hands in his pockets, shuffled toward them and halted at the foot of the steps. Darcy figured he was ten. His wheat-colored hair hung in clumps around his ears, and he looked and smelled as if he hadn't had a bath in weeks.

"This is Clint. I met him at the station in Raleigh—after I chased him down when he picked my pocket. He's an orphan and was sleeping in some crates in an alley. I told him he has a home here at the Refuge from now on."

"Of course he does," Charleigh said, brushing a tear from her eye. "Hello, Clint."

Darcy moved down the three steps and put out her hand. "Welcome to Lyons's Refuge."

The boy only stared back.

Darcy lowered her arm. "That's all right. You'll get used to us soon enough, I expect. Lyons's Refuge is a place like no other, you'll soon find." She laughed and looked toward the porch. "That's the schoolmaster, Mr. Thomas, and I'm the cook's assistant. You can call me Darcy. Do you like apple cake? I baked one this morning."

The boy shrugged. "Don't know. Ain't never et no cake before."

"Suh-fee!" a child's voice suddenly cried out. "Hi, Suh-fee!"

Everyone turned to look at the toddler in the open doorway. In her yellow frock, with her shiny, dark curls and big brown eyes, Angel looked as sweet as her name. Staring at Brent, she clapped her hands and jumped up and down, then fell to her frilled bottom.

From within the house an infant cried, the sound growing stronger. Alice walked out, a baby in her arms. "I think she wants you, Charleigh." Seeing Stewart, she stopped in surprise.

Stewart stared at the infant with bright red hair, then looked at his wife.

"Um, I also have someone I'd like for you to meet." Charleigh cleared her throat. "This is Clementine Marielle Lyons. Your daughter."

Stewart remained motionless, as though in a trance.

"Here now—would you like to hold her?" Alice asked. Before he could reply, she placed the baby in his arms.

Clemmie stopped crying and stared up at him, wide-eyed. Tears rolled down Stewart's cheeks. After a moment, he looked at Charleigh, his expression pained. "Why didn't you tell me? I never would've stayed away—"

Shaking her head, Charleigh pressed her fingers to his lips to stop his strangled words. "You're home now. That's all that matters. Let's put the past where it belongs—behind us."

Stewart gave a short nod and with his free arm drew her tightly to his side.

Angel toddled over to Brent and tugged on his jacket. "Suh-fee?"

"What *is* that child saying?" Stewart asked. "And who is she? Do we take in small girls now?"

Darcy laughed, returning to the porch, and scooped Angel up in her arms. "She's a friend's daughter, and she's saying Stuffy." She grinned up at her husband. "Somehow she got hold of that name for Brent and won't let go."

"Stuffy?" Stewart repeated.

"Suh-fee!" Angel squealed. She leaned over and threw her chubby arms around Brent's neck in a tight hug. They all laughed.

Stewart glanced at Brent. "Everything went well? No problems to report?"

Brent and Darcy shared a look. "Nothing we couldn't handle together," Brent said.

"Glad to hear it. You can fill me in on everything that's happened later. Right now I just want to relax and spend some time with my family. It's good to be home." With one arm around Charleigh and the other cradling his daughter, Stewart went inside. Angel kicked her legs to get down, and Darcy set her on the porch. She ran into the house, and Darcy and Brent moved to follow.

"Hey, Lady!" Clint yelled after them. "What about me?"

Darcy turned her head and grinned. "Well, what are you just standing there for? This is your home now too. Come on inside, and I'll get you a nice, thick slice of that cake."

This time the boy didn't hesitate. Wearing a bright smile, he was through the door faster than Darcy would have imagined it possible.

"He seems to have taken a liking to you," Brent said. "But then that comes as no surprise."

She grabbed his sleeve to stop him before he could follow the others. "Brent, about what you told Stewart—we do make a fine team, don't we?"

"Indubitably!"

Darcy arched her brow, determined to look up that word as soon as she could.

Brent laughed and tilted her chin up with his forefinger and thumb. "Most certainly," he clarified. "The very best." Bending down, he gave her a gentle kiss.

"Well, then," she whispered once he lifted his head, "would ye care to make it a threesome?"

"A threesome?" He looked puzzled.

Darcy smiled. "In eight months, I expect. Sometime around Clemmie's first birthday. How do ye feel about the name Beatrice? 'Course if it's a boy, he'd have to be Brent."

His eyes widened behind the spectacles, and his mouth dropped open. "Darcy, you don't mean. . ."

"I most certainly do! As long as everyone else is makin' introductions tonight, I might as well be makin' one of me own!"

She looped her arms around Brent's neck and kissed him soundly. From the side of the house, boys' snickering could be heard, but Darcy didn't mind.

Neither, it seemed, did Brent.

# A Letter To Our Readers

Dear Reader:

In order that we might better contribute to your reading enjoyment, we would appreciate your taking a few minutes to respond to the following questions. We welcome your comments and read each form and letter we receive. When completed, please return to the following:

Fiction Editor
Heartsong Presents
PO Box 719
Uhrichsville, Ohio 44683

1. Did you enjoy reading *Heart Appearances* by Pamela Griffin?
   ❏ Very much! I would like to see more books by this author!
   ❏ Moderately. I would have enjoyed it more if

   _____

   _____

   _____

2. Are you a member of **Heartsong Presents**? ❏ Yes ❏ No
   If no, where did you purchase this book? _____

   _____

3. How would you rate, on a scale from 1 (poor) to 5 (superior), the cover design? _____

4. On a scale from 1 (poor) to 10 (superior), please rate the following elements.

   ____ Heroine          ____ Plot
   ____ Hero             ____ Inspirational theme
   ____ Setting          ____ Secondary characters

5. These characters were special because?_____

_____

_____

6. How has this book inspired your life?_____

_____

_____

7. What settings would you like to see covered in future
   **Heartsong Presents** books? _____

_____

_____

8. What are some inspirational themes you would like to see
   treated in future books? _____

_____

_____

9. Would you be interested in reading other **Heartsong
   Presents** titles? ❏ Yes  ❏ No

10. Please check your age range:
    ❏ Under 18          ❏ 18-24
    ❏ 25-34             ❏ 35-45
    ❏ 46-55             ❏ Over 55

Name_____

Occupation_____

Address_____

City_____ State_____ Zip_____

# Gold Rush Christmas

## 4 stories in 1

GOLD RUSH CHRISTMAS

COLLEEN COBLE · REBECCA GERMANY
CATHY MARIE HAKE · JOYCE LIVINGSTON

*W*hen the "Gold Fever" epidemic sweeps the nation in 1849, people drop everything to chase the dream of striking it rich. Follow one family's itch for adventure from California to the Rockies to the Yukon—and discover a Christmas gift more valuable than gold.

Four Christmases in gold country prove life's most priceless gifts come not in the form of polished gold—but from the vast riches of a loving heart.

Historical, paperback, 352 pages, 5 3/16"x 8"

❤ ❤ ❤ ❤ ❤ ❤ ❤ ❤ ❤ ❤ ❤ ❤ ❤ ❤ ❤ ❤

❤ ❤ ❤ ❤ ❤ ❤ ❤ ❤ ❤ ❤ ❤ ❤ ❤ ❤ ❤ ❤

# ------- **Presents** -------